She's won the hearts of readers
her unforgettable stories of love, including
Eye of the Beholder, Elusive Dawn,
and *On Her Doorstep* . . .
Now NATIONAL BESTSELLING AUTHOR
KAY HOOPER
captures the sparkling, magnetic force that brings
two hearts together, the explosive chemistry of
lovers who know each other too well—and who
know they can't stay away . . .

Return Engagement

Devlin shrugged into his robe and belted it securely,
then reached down for the bikini. Holding the scraps of
material negligently in two fingers, he turned to smile at
her, deviltry gleaming in his eyes. "Come and get it," he
invited gently. His voice was filled with laughter, and
Tara's temper flared once again.

"If you were a gentleman—"

"Well, I'm not, so there's no use telling me what I'd do
if that were the case. Come out of there."

As she reached him, Devlin swung the large towel
behind her and hesitated, his eyes sweeping over her
again. Then he slowly pulled the ends of the towel toward
him until she stepped closer, and they were separated only
by the fabric of his robe. Bending his head, he whispered
huskily, "Lady, you are really testing my willpower."

Praise for *The Matchmaker* by Kay Hooper:

"[An] overwhelming love story . . . filled with passion . . .
outstanding!"   —*Rendezvous*

RETURN ENGAGEMENT

KAY HOOPER

Originally published under the
pseudonym Kay Robbins

JOVE BOOKS, NEW YORK

This Jove Book contains the complete
text of the original edition.

RETURN ENGAGEMENT

A Jove Book / published by arrangement with
the author

PRINTING HISTORY
Originally was published in the Second Chance
at Love series in September 1982
Jove edition / January 1995

ISBN: 0-515-11525-8

A JOVE BOOK®
Jove Books are published by The Berkley Publishing Group,
200 Madison Avenue, New York, New York 10016.
JOVE and the "J" design are trademarks
belonging to Jove Publications, Inc.

PRINTED IN THE UNITED STATES OF AMERICA

10 9 8 7 6 5 4 3 2 1

For Jewel—
A friend indeed . . .

Chapter 1

"*You're* off your mark, Miss Collins!"

The harsh voice scraped across Tara's nerves like fingernails on a blackboard, and she resisted an impulse to scream in sheer frustration. It was the third time Bradley had interrupted the rehearsal—and he wasn't even the director, for heaven's sake! Whirling to confront her tormentor, she shouted, "I was *not* off my mark! This is exactly where Derek told me to stand!"

The big, casually dressed man who was leaning easily against the low wall of the veranda a few feet away returned her glare with a cutting smile. "But he didn't tell you to plaster yourself all over Gallows like a second skin. This isn't an X-rated film, Miss Collins. Force yourself to remember that."

Tara made a choked sound that was half a gasp of outrage and half a smothered oath. "You've got a

hell of a nerve!" she managed to say at last, her blue
eyes shooting sparks of rage and embarrassment.
How dare he speak to her like that in front of all
these people! "Get your mind out of the gutter,
Mr. Bradley. This is supposed to be a love scene—
which you'd know if you'd read the script—and I
did *not* plaster myself all over Randy!"

Bradley laughed briefly. "From where I'm standing, Miss Collins, you looked like an advertisement
for a red-light district."

"I'm sure you'd know what *that* looks like," she
retorted nastily, and was immediately angry at herself for turning the criticism into a personal remark.
And *why* couldn't she tear her eyes away from his
lean body? Reading the gleam in his silvery eyes,
she saw that he was about to reply to her remark,
and spoke quickly to head him off. "Just because
you're backing this film doesn't give you the right
to stand around criticizing everything we do!"

His wide shoulders lifted in a shrug. "I have to
protect my investment, Miss Collins," he returned
coolly. "And that investment does, in fact, give me
the right to criticize. I'd also like to point out that
my money pays your salary."

"So?" she demanded.

"So watch yourself, Miss Collins," he told her in
a silky tone that didn't quite hide the steel. "As
much as I enjoy crossing swords with you, there
comes a time in every match when one opponent
must concede defeat."

"Oh? Are you waving the white flag already?"
she asked with sweet innocence.

He shifted slightly, impatiently, and Tara found
her eyes once again drawn to his powerful body. "I

hold the upper hand in this match, Tara, and you know it," he snapped.

Tara sensed heads turning and ears pricking as the cast and crew noticed Bradley's lapse from formal address to the use of her first name. Furious with him for stepping over the line she had drawn between them three years before, she bit out coldly, "Your ego defies description, *Mr.* Bradley! Don't be so damned sure of yourself!"

His silver-gray eyes narrowed sharply, and Tara knew he understood the reason for the sudden intensity of her anger. Before he could take yet another step across the invisible line separating them, she put the conversation firmly back on a professional footing.

"Mr. Bradley," she began, in a sweet tone expressly calculated to drive a saint to murder, "why were all of us hired?"

Arms folded over his massive chest, Bradley smiled across at her, his even white teeth reminding Tara of a wolf on the prowl. "I should think you'd know the answer to that, *Miss* Collins. You've been in the business long enough."

Her teeth came together with an audible snap. "Look, you complained not three days ago that we were behind schedule and over budget. Don't you think we'd finish this picture a lot faster if you didn't drive out here every day just to interfere?"

Tara was just beginning to work up a good head of steam, and she relished the feeling. "If you think you can do everything so much better than us, then do it!" she invited acidly. "Handle the cameras, direct the picture, even star in it! But you're going to have a hell of a time fitting into my costume!"

Her slender hands indicated the silk dress she was wearing, which clung flatteringly to every inch of her lush body.

"Finished?" Bradley inquired courteously.

"Only if you're leaving." She glared at him.

"I'm not leaving."

"Then I'm not finished!" She took a deep breath and gave her temper full rein. "I'll admit that this is a good part, but I have better things to do than stand around in the desert and listen to you snipe at me!"

One dark brow lifted sardonically. "Are you threatening to walk out, Miss Collins?"

"Oh, you'd like that, wouldn't you? Well, I'm not about to break my contract, Mr. Bradley. If you don't like the way I'm handling this part, fire me!"

"Keep it up, Miss Collins, and I just might." His deep voice was a little grim.

Elated at having finally goaded him, Tara opened her mouth to prod him a bit more, hoping that he'd get angry enough to leave them in peace, but she was forestalled by her obviously worried costar.

"Tara, why don't we take a little break while Derek gets set up for this scene?" Randy suggested hastily. "It's been a long morning. I'm sure Mr. Bradley understands that we're all tired—"

"You stay out of this!" Bradley interrupted fiercely, his silver eyes shooting metallic sparks in a dangerous warning. "You're not up to her weight!"

"Neither are you!" Tara snapped back. From the corner of her eye she saw Randy throw up his hands in defeat and retire to the opposite side of the veranda. Then she forgot about him. She was too wrapped up in writing another chapter in her years-long feud with the annoying Devlin Bradley. "And stop ordering people around!" she added for good measure.

"I sign the paychecks, spitfire. That gives me the right to order people around."

Irritably Tara wondered why that particular insult sounded more like an endearment from an amused and indulgent lover. She began heatedly, "You can take your paycheck and—"

"Fifteen minutes, people," Derek, the director, intervened hastily, rising from his chair, "then we'll shoot the scene."

Tara turned to him, but when Derek met her glare with a wry plea in his eyes, she gave up. Stalking over to the farthest corner of the veranda, she found a spot in the shade and sat down in a wicker chair. She was hoping that her abrupt change of mood had angered Devlin Bradley, but when she glanced his way she found him strolling over to talk to one of the cameramen.

Irritated, she watched Derek approach her with the watchful, wary gaze of a man whose pet kitten has suddenly turned into a lioness, and her sense of humor abruptly righted itself. Grimacing apologetically, she murmured, "Sorry, Derek—but he makes me so mad." With effort, she kept her voice low.

"No—really?" Derek leaned against the low wall beside Randy and gave her a look of comical surprise. "Well, now, I never would have guessed that if you hadn't pointed it out."

"It must be her red hair," Randy murmured thoughtfully.

"No, I think it's Bradley," Derek disagreed in a contemplative tone, for all the world as though Tara were invisible. "There must be something peculiar in his chemistry. Or hers. Every time they're within ten feet of each other, the sparks start flying."

"Hey!" Tara waved a hand to attract their attention. "I'm here, you know. Don't talk about me as if I weren't."

Derek and Randy exchanged looks, and then Derek looked down at Tara with the same wry plea in his eyes. "Honey, we only have two scenes to go, and then we can all leave this damned desert. Do you think you can put a rein on that temper of yours for the rest of the day? You're twenty-six years old. You should be able to control it by now."

"Bradley's thirty-six—why can't he control *his* temper?" Tara asked mutinously.

Randy lifted a sandy brow, his rugged face curious. "How do you know how old he is, Tara?"

Tara felt a flush rise in her cheeks, but forced herself to look calm. "How do you think? If he so much as sneezes it makes the papers. His life's no secret."

Randy nodded absently, watching as Derek was called over to settle a slight dispute between two of the technicians. "How did you meet him, Tara? I've been wondering."

"At a premiere party a few years ago," she replied in an offhand manner. "I had a small part in the picture he backed." She stared across to where Bradley was talking to Derek, and grimaced irritably. "Just look at him," she muttered, forgetting her audience. "Not so much as a drop of sweat to prove he's human. And he never loses control. Never. Just once I'd like to see him really blow his stack."

"I wouldn't," Randy said flatly. "Not unless I had a concrete bunker to hide in, anyway. Devlin Bradley strikes me as the sort of man it doesn't pay to rile." He grinned suddenly. "But you just go right on stoking the fire, don't you, Tara? Do you have a death wish?"

With just the right touch of scorn in her voice, Tara responded, "The man is arrogant, egotistical, domineering, and rude. I'm not going to fawn all over him just because everyone else does." She wondered vaguely why she couldn't put such a disagreeable man out of her mind, and why her pulse rate increased so frantically whenever she saw him or heard his voice. It had been three years, for goodness sake!

"Not a member of his fan club, are you?" Randy was asking in an amused tone.

"You could say that," Tara agreed dryly. "His fan club is full of adoring women."

"God knows you'd never be mistaken for one of *those*." Randy laughed. "Tell me something, Tara—did you hate him at first sight, or did it take a year or so for the feelings to build?"

"Oh, at first sight," she replied airily. "The only thing we've ever agreed on is the fact that we can't stand each other." She looked up at him with an easy smile, succeeding at last in tearing her eyes away from Bradley.

"And you've been fighting ever since then?" Randy asked curiously.

"Ever since." Tara changed the subject determinedly. "What's this I hear about a possible engagement for you?"

Randy grimaced slightly. "You've been reading the gossip columns. I only went out with the lady twice, and the press has me engaged to her." In almost the same breath he went on casually, "I wonder if the stories of Bradley's love life are exaggerated. What do you think?"

"I think it's none of my business." Swearing silently at Randy's persistence in talking about her own personal nemesis, Tara managed nonetheless to keep her voice calm.

Ignoring her apparent disinterest, Randy said thoughtfully, "That model he's been seen with for the past few months seems to have the inside track as far as he's concerned. I've even heard whispers of a wedding. That article last month—"

"I read it," Tara interrupted firmly, her mind's eye filling with the image of the gorgeous blonde who had been hanging on Bradley's arm in public with increasing frequency. Pushing the oddly disturbing picture away, she looked up and nodded to acknowledge Derek's signal, then went on smoothly, "Let's go, champ—Derek's ready for us."

To Tara's relief, Randy abandoned his speculation about Bradley and followed her across the veranda to their marks. This time the scene came off without a hitch. Tara wasn't completely satisfied with her performance—she felt a little stiff in Randy's arms after Bradley's earlier remark—but Derek seemed delighted, so she left well enough alone. The cast and crew immediately dispersed for lunch, some heading for cars and the drive to Vegas, some heading for the cool interior of the bungalow or the trailers, parked a few yards away.

Tara headed for her air-conditioned trailer. She wasn't really hungry, and a brief, stabbing pain between her eyes warned her that she needed to get out of the sun.

"Tara."

With one hand on the trailer door she turned in surprise to watch Bradley approach her. A swift glance showed her that no one was close enough to overhear them, but she still wasn't happy about being alone with him. Experience had taught her that with Devlin Bradley around, she was safer in a crowd. "Yes?" she asked haughtily.

Apparently undisturbed by her quelling question, he halted a short distance away and looked at her with unreadable eyes. "I'm driving in to Vegas for lunch," he said calmly. "Come with me?"

Her fingers tightened on the door handle. "No." She hesitated, then added a grudging, "Thank you."

"Such pretty manners," he mocked softly, and then added, with a faint twist of his lips, "Still afraid someone will think you're in cahoots with the boss?"

Tara stiffened, her blue eyes flashing with anger. "You've never forgiven me for that, have you?" she asked stonily. "It dented your ego to think that I preferred my independence to your . . . protection."

He slid his hands into the pockets of his close-fitting black pants and continued to regard her with an unreadable expression. "My ego," he murmured thoughtfully. "Yes, I suppose it did dent my ego. But I offered more than protection, Tara." The silvery eyes raked over her, from her short red curls to her sandal-clad feet, without missing an inch along the way. "I offered marriage."

She smiled bitterly. "And I was supposed to be delighted that you'd decided to make an honest woman of me? No way, Devlin. I'd rather be dishonest."

"Really?" He lifted a mocking brow. "Well, they say there's a streak of the harlot in every woman."

Tara took a hasty step toward him, her face white and her eyes blazing. Anger and bitterness combined to form an icy ball in the pit of her stomach, and the stabbing pain between her eyes increased with the force of her emotions.

Before she could utter the scathing words on her tongue, Devlin said, "I'm sorry." His lean face wore an expression of self-contempt, brief but real. "That was uncalled-for, I know."

"But not totally unexpected." She smiled tightly. "You don't pull any punches, do you, Devlin?"

His remarkable eyes had darkened to a cloudy gray, suddenly somber. "Not with you. But then, we've always been brutally honest with each other, haven't we, Tara?"

"Brutally," she agreed in a flat tone.

After a moment, he said dryly, "Then be honest with me now. Why won't you have lunch with me?"

She hesitated. "I'm not hungry."

Devlin laughed shortly. "If you were starving you wouldn't have lunch with me, would you?"

Her mouth curved in a sudden, mocking smile. "If I were starving I just might. But then, if I were starving I'd have lunch with the devil himself."

"Thanks!" He shifted impatiently. "After three years of your brand of warfare it's a wonder I have any ego at all."

Tara crossed her arms over her breasts and leaned back against the trailer door, staring at him wryly. "You have what they call 'total ego,' Devlin. You know exactly who you are and who you're not, and no one's opinion is going to change that."

"Well, *that* makes me sound lovable as hell!"

"There are a lot of adjectives I could use to describe you," she told him sweetly, "but 'lovable' isn't one of them."

He stared at her for a moment and then grinned suddenly. "That must be one of the reasons I keep hanging around, Tara. You keep me on my toes," he said ruefully. "Pax, huh? Have lunch with me."

Tara swore silently at the faintly pleading look in his eyes, reflecting bitterly that when Devlin turned on the charm, he was incredibly hard to resist. And he knew it, damn him! That smile could charm the devil out of hell, and Devlin used it ruthlessly to get his own way. But not this time. She'd fallen for that smile once, and remembered all too well the heartache it had caused.

"I'm not hungry."

His smile disappeared. "The years haven't changed you, Tara. You're still as stubborn as ever."

"Nothing's changed, Devlin." She looked him squarely in the eye. "Nothing at all."

He nodded slowly, still staring at her. "Yes. Yes, I'm beginning to see that." His silvery eyes reflected a new concern. Almost to himself, he murmured, "You're thin as a rail."

Tara started at the abrupt change of subject and then lied stoutly. "I'm on a diet." She felt torn between irritation and pleasure that he had noticed her weight loss. Irritation won. "Not that it's any of your business," she snapped.

The worry in his eyes spread, until he was scowling slightly. "That's stupid, Tara," he said harshly. "You don't need to lose weight. If anything, you need to gain it. And you're as tense as a drawn bow. What are you trying to do, make yourself sick?"

Relieved that they were back on angry footing, where she felt more secure, she responded flatly, "My appearance is my own business, and I'll thank you to remember that!" Before he could utter a word, she had entered the trailer and slammed the door.

Inside, leaning against the door, Tara glanced around the cozy interior of her motor home and thought vaguely that there was nothing like slamming a door to make a woman feel vindicated.

"Waurr!"

She looked down to see her Siamese cat sitting at her feet, one chocolate-colored paw clamped firmly over the tail of a struggling, indignantly squeaking mouse.

"No, Ah Poo," Tara told him flatly. "You can't go out and play. The heat out there would broil you alive. And let Churchill go!"

With a snort peculiar to Siamese cats, Ah Poo released his reluctant toy and watched with indifferent, slightly crossed china-blue eyes as the mouse scurried frantically for the safety of a pair of Tara's shoes, on the floor beside the couch.

Tara leaned over to fish him out, holding him in one hand and absently stroking his tiny head as she stared cautiously through the window beside the door. Devlin was striding toward the bungalow, his stiff shoulders visible evidence of his anger. Apparently he had decided not to drive to Vegas after all.

With a faint sigh Tara turned away from the window and carried the mouse over to a small cage on a low table. Placing Churchill inside, she sank down on the couch and frowned at her cat. "Ah Poo, if you let him out of his cage one more time, I'm going to buy a padlock. You hear me?"

She smiled slightly as Ah Poo merely stared at her. Then she leaned back and rubbed fretfully at the point of stabbing pain between her eyes. She tried to forget Devlin's charming smile. . . .

The rest of the afternoon crept by with agonizing slowness. Nothing went right. The major problem, Tara decided by four o'clock, was Devlin Bradley, who was making his presence felt with a vengeance. He was obviously in a lousy mood, and taking it out on everybody—particularly Tara. When he verbally lambasted her acting for the sixth time, she began entertaining thoughts of homicide.

She was honestly afraid that if she said a word to him, it would lead to murder—his. Finally she collapsed into a chair on the veranda and tried to get a grip on her raging temper. The pain between her eyes had become a blinding agony, and she only half saw Derek coming toward her. He was frowning.

He leaned against the low wall beside her and smiled sympathetically. "Shall we take up a collection and hire a hit man?" he asked ruefully.

Tara managed a weary smile. "You don't have to do that. I'll pay the whole tab. All I ask is the pleasure of watching him get it."

Derek grinned. "You look as though you've already gone ten rounds with him." He gestured at Tara's costume, which was mostly rags—jeans and a cotton top. The scene they were trying to film dramatized her return from a terrifying night alone in the desert.

Tara leaned her chin on one hand and stared grimly across to where Devlin was berating one of the cameramen. "How does one hire a hit man, anyway?" she asked absently. "That would solve all our problems." When the silence remained unbroken, she looked up to find Derek frowning at her.

"Do you feel okay?" he asked slowly. "Your color's not right."

"A headache, that's all." She shrugged. "And you didn't answer my question. How does one go about hiring a hit man? I don't think they move in my circles."

"It's not exactly something they taught me in director's school," Derek responded dryly. He hesitated for a moment, then went on casually, "You wait here. I think I'll go and have a word with the man. Be right back."

As he rose to his feet, Tara warned, "Better speak softly and carry a big stick. That's the only kind of conversation 'the man' understands."

Derek grinned and left her. Tara leaned her head against the back of her chair. With her eyelids drooping to cut out most of the glare from the fiery sun, she acknowledged to herself that she should have passed this picture by and taken a vacation. She had been lucky to have work for the past three years, to be too busy to take more than a brief rest between projects. Now she had a sneaking suspicion that her body was warning her to slow down... or else.

She always found it difficult to work on one of Devlin's films, because their constant and often heated arguments drained the energy she needed for her work. But over the years she had learned to cope. Or at least she thought she had. Now she wasn't so sure. Why did she feel so tired?

"Can't you handle a prima donna, Derek?"

The sneering voice brought Tara upright with a jerk. Across the veranda her eyes met the searing brightness of Devlin's mocking gaze. Almost at once she realized that Derek had tried to postpone production—probably for her sake—and that Devlin thought she was faking an illness.

That one phrase—prima donna—was all it took to send the adrenaline flowing through her veins once again. She jumped to her feet, cheeks flushed with anger and eyes glittering. "I'm ready to shoot the scene, Derek," she called.

"We're all tired—" Derek began.

"Then, the sooner we wrap this scene, the sooner we can all go home," Tara cut in ruthlessly. "I'm ready when you are."

Derek shot an angry look at Devlin, then nodded reluctantly and stalked toward the cameras. "Let's go, people!" he shouted.

Without glancing at Devlin, Tara headed out into the desert to where the cameras would pick her up. With the ease of long practice she cleared her mind of everything except the character she was portraying and silently reviewed her lines.

Five minutes later the cameras were rolling and Tara was stumbling across a harsh, unfriendly desert. She was a woman alone, abandoned by her lover to live or die, her strength sapped by terror and heartache. She had risked everything for love, pinned her trust and faith on a man as cold and fickle as the stars, and he had left her raw and bleeding.

Lurching, falling, picking herself up to stagger on, her blue eyes were fixed on the looming bungalow with a hopelessness and desperation that teetered on the brink of madness. Tears cleaned furrows down her dirty cheeks. Her breath came in harsh rasps.

Stumbling the last few yards, she leaned against the low wall of the veranda and in a hoarse voice called out the name of her lover, knowing all the while that he wouldn't answer. He didn't. Sobbing in pain and exhaustion, she gripped the wall with white-knuckled fingers and cursed his name bitterly. And then a scream of sheer agony ripped from her throat, and she slid down the wall to stare across the unfeeling desert landscape with bleak, empty eyes. "Damn you," she murmured weakly, raggedly. "Damn you to hell . . ."

There was a long silence. Then Derek yelled, "Cut! Print it!"

Tara swallowed the sick feeling in her throat and painfully rose slowly to her feet, wondering vaguely why the scenery around her seemed to be swaying crazily. As if from far away she heard the crew burst into spontaneous applause. But her eyes passed by them to search out Devlin Bradley. He stood apart from the others, his arms folded across his chest. Their eyes locked, and the expression of respect in his steady gaze was the last thing Tara saw before she began to fall. And then blackness overwhelmed her.

Chapter 2

Tara was dimly aware of many voices speaking at once, of hands touching her gently, of someone harshly, urgently calling her name. But it seemed too difficult to respond. Her hearing kept fading in and out. She was vaguely aware that someone was issuing a great many orders in a commanding voice. The sound irritated her, although she didn't know why.

And then she was floating. The sound of distant, steady thunder echoed in her ears, and the confusion of many voices faded away. Something warm and smelling of a curiously familiar spicy scent was wrapped around her. She felt safe and cared for.

Dreams came and went. Some were absurd dreams of talking animals and spaceships and people with wacky personalities. Some were nightmares—a rat's maze, a dark cave, a house with hundreds of rooms and no windows. Thunder rumbled and lightning flashed, making her cringe in terror. She wanted to call out to someone, but the name would not form in her clouded mind.

Finally the dreams faded away into darkness. More than once she was conscious of her hand's being pressed gently, of something brushing her cheeks, her forehead. Faint echoes of voices— some calm, some harsh and demanding—touched her dimly, as if from a great distance. And then everything became peaceful.

She woke from time to time, dimly aware that she was in a hospital room but not really troubled by it. Often someone was by her bed, a comforting presence she didn't try to identify. She woke once to find the presence gone, and felt restless and uneasy until it returned, crying out fretfully against the unfamiliar voices trying to calm her. After that the presence was always there.

Several times she found herself in a dreamy, half-awake state, conscious of lights and shadows and the scent of roses. Voices were more distinct now, and she was able to catch snatches of conversation going on around her. The conversation wasn't very interesting. Two men seemed to be talking about someone who was ill. She roused herself enough to mutter to them to go away and leave her in peace, and was answered with a huskily amused laugh from a voice that sounded vaguely familiar.

At first it took a great effort to struggle to regain semiconsciousness. The demands of her body for rest were too strong to fight. Slowly, though, she realized that she was sleeping only because she wanted to, not because she had to. Her workaholic nature immediately rebelled at that thought. What was she doing in a hospital, anyway? She wasn't sick. And she had a picture to do in just a few weeks. She couldn't afford to lie around in a hospital bed all day.

Irritated with herself, and at whoever had officiously stuck her in here, Tara opened her eyes. She felt wide awake and reasonably fit, a little tired, perhaps—but that was only to be expected. She had been working hard, after all.

Sunlight filled the room and fell across vases of flowers lining a low chest by the door. Tara decided absently that she must have slept all night. Her eyes followed the shafts of light across the room to the window, falling at last on the man standing there.

His dark hair was a bit rumpled, his coat discarded and lying over a chair in the corner. The stark masculinity of his profile was etched for her in the light shining through the window—a high, intelligent forehead, an aquiline nose, a firm-lipped mouth. The strong jaw was shadowed with at least a day's growth of beard. Sleepy lids hid a pair of eyes that, she knew, were of such a light gray as to appear silver. Hard, keen eyes that could—but only rarely did—glow with molten fire.

At five feet eight inches tall, Tara was not a small woman, but the man standing before the window had always possessed the power to make her feel small. It might have been his own size—he was six feet four inches and built like a football player—or it might have been the sheer force of his personality. One glance from those silvery eyes warned her that he was a man to be reckoned with.

And Tara knew that well. Oh, yes—she knew that very well.

She watched him for a long time, secure in the knowledge that he was unaware she had awakened. It was a rare opportunity to study him unobserved, and Tara was appalled by just how much she wanted to look at him. Not for the first time, she wondered if she had been wrong three years ago when she had refused to give up her career for him.

It wouldn't have worked out, she assured herself miserably. She was an actress, dammit, not a little housewife. She immediately amended the unfair thought. She wouldn't have been a "little housewife," and she knew it. Just another business wife, bored to tears at business dinner-parties and listening to other business wives talk about who was sleeping with whom and the shocking cost of decorators.

It wasn't as if he'd given her a good reason to abandon her career for marriage. He hadn't even mentioned love, for instance. Or children. In fact, he'd given her no reason at all to suppose that she would have been anything more than a bird in a gilded cage. And be it ever so lovely or comfortably furnished, a cage was still a cage. What was she supposed to do—sit around all day filing her nails?

Why had he wanted to marry her, anyway? Probably, she decided irritably, because he had grown tired of having women chase him. And since she'd been the first one in line, she had received the offer.

Angry at her thoughts, Tara turned her eyes to the ceiling. It was done. Over. There was no reason to think about it any longer.

"How do you feel?"

Blinking, she discovered that Devlin was standing by the bed, staring down at her with unreadable eyes. She turned her gaze back to the ceiling and answered flatly, "Like I've been run over by a truck—twice. Were you driving it?" From the corner of her eye, she saw his face tighten.

"In a manner of speaking." He pulled a chair forward and sank into it. "Dammit, Tara, why did you do it?"

The outburst startled her. Without thinking, she turned her head to stare at him blankly.

"Why did you let me goad you into driving yourself too hard?" he demanded harshly.

Irritated, she responded evenly, "What did you expect me to do after you called me a prima donna?"

"I didn't know you were really ill."

"Have I *ever*," she shot back coldly, "held up production with a fake illness?"

His lips formed a tight line. "No. But you were angry enough that day to fake an illness. You should have—"

"What do you mean 'that day'?" she interrupted. "You talk as if it were days ago."

He stared at her for a moment. "It was. You collapsed the day before yesterday."

She was shocked, but tried to hide it by murmuring, "I was just a little tired, that's all. I must have needed the sleep."

"A little tired?" Devlin shook his head, looking grim. "You were exhausted—pure and simple. The doctor said you should have taken a long vacation months ago. Stupid little fool."

The last comment, apparently tacked on as an afterthought, did nothing for Tara's uncertain temper. "I'm neither stupid nor little," she informed him irritably. "Stop treating me like a child."

"Then stop acting like one! For God's sake, Tara, anyone with a grain of sense would have realized what was happening. I'm beginning to believe you need a keeper."

"You've thought that all along," she snapped, tears welling up in her eyes. She was immediately angry with him for being present to witness her unusual weakness.

Reaching over to cover one of her restless hands with his, Devlin said quietly, "You're experiencing the aftereffects of the exhaustion, Tara. The doctor said you won't feel like yourself for a while. Don't be afraid."

Tara wasn't particularly surprised by his seeming ability to read her mind, because he'd often displayed that uncanny knack in the past. But his gentleness disturbed her, and his touch brought back memories she wanted badly to forget. Snatching her hand away, she muttered tightly, "Why are you here, Devlin? Guilty conscience?"

He sat back in his chair with a frown. After a moment his lids dropped to veil his eyes, and he responded coolly, "I was the only one without commitments elsewhere. The others stayed as long as they could, though. Derek and Randy have called every day to check on you, and the whole production crew sent flowers." He nodded toward the colorful offerings on either side of the door.

"That was kind of them." A sudden thought made Tara's eyes widen in horror. "Ah Poo! What—"

"It's all right," Devlin interrupted calmly. "I've got him at my apartment." He grinned suddenly. "Randy had the noble intention of taking the cat to L.A. and keeping him for you, but after Ah Poo nearly scratched his eyes out, he decided to let me take care of the problem. Ah Poo's fine."

Tara looked at him wryly. "I don't suppose you explained to Randy why the cat happens to like you?"

Devlin shrugged. "If you mean did I tell him that I gave you a Siamese kitten three years ago, no. I just told him that the cat obviously had good taste."

Typical Devlin, she thought, and then frowned. "Are we still in Vegas? I didn't know you had an apartment here."

"I don't. A friend of mine does, though."

"I see." Tara thought that she did see, and she was angered by the jealousy that that lanced through her.

With a peculiarly satisfied smile, Devlin said dryly, "A *male* friend, Tara. Jim's in Europe for the summer."

The blush that Tara had never been able to control reddened her cheeks. "I don't care if you have a harem in that apartment," she snapped defensively.

"Well, I don't," he responded calmly. "Just an unhappy housekeeper, a temperamental feline, and a mouse in a padlocked cage."

Tara felt tears rise to her eyes again. "You—you've got Churchill too?"

"Sure. Randy told me about him, and Ah Poo found him for me. When Jim's housekeeper climbed down off a chair for the third time and threatened to quit—also for the third time—I bought a cage and a padlock. Mrs. Henson is happy these days, but Ah Poo's frustrated as hell."

Picturing the whole scene, Tara smiled at him. Devlin's gaze dropped immediately to her mouth. Huskily, he murmured, "That's the first time you've really smiled at me since . . ." His voice trailed away.

Tara immediately returned her gaze to the ceiling, silently damning herself for that unguarded smile. She was in no shape to cope with Devlin Bradley right now, and she knew it. More than anything in the world she wanted him to walk out the door and out of her life. She was afraid of what would happen to her if he stayed.

"Why did we split up, Tara?"

The quiet question made her heart skip a beat, and she willed herself sternly not to look at him. "You know very well why."

"Because you had the fixed idea that if you landed a role in a film—especially one of *my* films—it would be because of our relationship and not your own talent? Because you believed I interfered in your career? Because I asked you to give up your career?"

"All of the above," she answered flippantly.

"You were wrong," he said quietly, ignoring her don't-give-a-damn attitude. "Your talent is too well known for anyone but a fool to believe you'd earned your roles on your back."

Tara winced at the blunt statement. "You have such a delicate way with words."

"Why wrap it up in euphemisms? That was what you were afraid of, wasn't it?"

"Present tense, Devlin." She turned to stare at him bitterly. "That's what I *am* afraid of. I won't be labeled an easy conquest, and I won't be accused of trading on my looks or my relationships with anyone in the industry. I'm an actress. An *actress*. And that's the only way I'll be judged."

"You've already proven that, Tara."

"And I'll have to go on proving it every day. There's a double standard, Devlin, and you know it as well as I do. As long as an actress is hired for her talent, then everything is fine. But it takes only a whisper of casting couch for her career to topple. I won't take that chance."

"You're being paranoid."

"No, *you're* being unrealistic."

A certain grimness had crept into his face, and there was an expression in his eyes that she couldn't quite fathom. It looked almost like anxiety, but Tara knew that couldn't be right. It didn't make sense. Devlin was never anxious. Never.

"Okay," he said slowly, "let's skip that for the moment and go on to the other reasons we split up."

"There's no need to discuss it." Tara moved restlessly in the bed, wishing she had the strength to get up and run away. She didn't want to open old wounds. "It's been dead for three years, Devlin. Why rake over the ashes?"

"Is it dead, Tara? Is it really?"

Suddenly he was sitting on the edge of the bed, staring down at her with silver flames in his eyes. Tara tried to look away, but the magnetic pull of his gaze held her as if in a trap. She was powerless to move even when his hands came out to gently

brush aside the loose hospital gown until he found
the delicate bones of her shoulders. Striving for
some kind of sanity, she said weakly, "It's dead.
It *is!*"

Devlin didn't waste time with words. Even as his
dark head bent toward her, Tara felt her own lips
parting in a helpless acknowledgment of a need too
long denied. The touch of his mouth was a searing
brand, setting fire to her delusion of having gotten over him. That hard-won belief crumbled into
ashes.

Tara felt his tongue probing gently along the sensitive inner surface of her lips, pleading for rather
than insisting on a response. The fire of that silent
request acted on her body like a torch. She told
herself that her illness was excuse enough for her
arms to curl around the strong brown column of
his neck, that she was obviously addled in the head
and in no condition to resist him. Then, having
made peace with her conscience, she gave herself
up totally to the familiar magic of his touch.

As her mouth blossomed beneath his, Devlin
deepened the kiss, his hands moving up to touch her
face, her throat. His touch conveyed a hot demand,
a hunger that was ravenous in its intensity. It was
as if he had been starving for three long years.

The same hunger blossomed within Tara. That
deeply buried, carefully hidden part of herself rose
to the surface now, as it had always done before,
frightening her with its turbulent, aching need. It
was not simply a need for his possession—although
that was certainly part of it—but a restless yearning
for something she had never been able to put a
name to. And could not now. She knew only that

no other man had the power to touch her as deeply as Devlin did.

His lips left hers to trail across her cheek, one hand sliding down to warmly cup her breast through the thin hospital gown. Tara arched involuntarily against him as she felt the dizzying sensations of his thumb brushing across her nipple and his teeth toying gently with her earlobe. A shaking gasp left her throat. Dimly she was aware of his husky whisper.

"Tara, honey, I want you so badly. It's been hell without you. Stop fighting me, sweetheart."

Caught up in the wild, sweet passion her body remembered so well, Tara made no attempt to fight him. She locked her fingers in his thick, dark hair and pulled his mouth back to hers, welcoming his heavy weight as he leaned fully on top of her.

"Excuse me . . . please."

The dry, laughter-filled voice jerked them apart like puppets on a string. Her cheeks nearly as red as her hair, Tara looked past Devlin's retreating body to see a young doctor whose brown eyes were twinkling merrily. Embarrassment and rage swept over her, and she glared at both men as Devlin straightened casually and raked a hand through the thick hair that her passionate fingers had disarranged.

"Hi, Doc," he said laconically.

If there had been a vase within reach, or a rock, or a club—anything!—Tara would have mustered her strength and done her damndest to brain him. How dared he stand there as calmly as though nothing had happened. How *dared* he! Of all the sneaky, low-down, underhanded tricks—to take advantage of a sick woman. Because, of course, she never would have responded to him if she'd been well . . .

The injustice of that last thought brought a rueful frown to Tara's face, and she shot a glare at Devlin that promised great things along the lines of revenge.

The young doctor came across the room to the bed, smiling apologetically. "I really didn't mean to interrupt. I'm Dr. Easton. How are you feeling, Miss Collins?"

With a very sweet smile Tara replied, "I feel weak, Doctor . . . and very unlike myself." The remark was meant solely for Devlin, and Tara felt a glimmer of satisfaction when she caught his wry smile from the corner of her eye.

"That's to be expected, Miss Collins." Dr. Easton was clearly unaware of any double meaning. "You've had a rough time of it. It'll take awhile for your body to recover its strength. Your fiancé has been telling us about your tendency to push yourself too hard."

Fiancé? What in the world—? Tara opened her mouth to voice her angry questions aloud, but a motion from the corner of her eye caught her attention. Glancing sideways, she saw Devlin give his head a tiny shake, clear warning in his eyes. Oh, God, what had he gotten her into this time? she asked herself wildly.

The doctor continued cheerfully, unconscious of his patient's perturbation. "The human body is a wonderful thing, Miss Collins, but it does have its limits. I'd say you reached yours a good two months ago. You're going to have to learn to slow down."

Tara shifted restlessly beneath the covers. "I'm trying to build a career, Doctor. I don't have time to slow down. How soon can I go back to work? I have a major role in a picture due to begin filming next month."

Easton was shaking his head. "Unless you want to end up right back in the hospital, Miss Collins, you'd better postpone that for a while. At least for a couple of months."

"But . . . the film," she protested, "can't be postponed! Doctor, they won't wait for me. They'll find someone else to do the part. I can't afford to let that happen."

Devlin spoke for the first time, his voice rueful. "I warned you, Doc. She's as stubborn as she is beautiful."

Not the least impressed by the backhanded compliment, Tara glared at him. "You stay out of this!" she warned irritably. "I'm not going to let the best part of my life slip by just because I'm a little tired."

If Easton was surprised by Tara's treatment of her fiancé, he didn't show it. With a trace of a professional chill in his voice, he said calmly, "You'll do as you please, of course, Miss Collins. But if you ignore my advice, your next collapse will prove to be far more serious."

Tara felt Devlin's hand come out to cover hers. She neither questioned the silent reassurance nor withdrew from it. "I see," she said softly.

Easton glanced across the bed at Devlin, then said quietly, "I know it won't be easy for you to do nothing, Miss Collins. From what I understand, you've been one of the busiest actresses in Hollywood during the past few years. But you'd better stop to consider something. Movies are a dime a dozen, but you've only got one body. Don't wear it out."

Tara was tempted to ask him what bad movie he'd gotten those lines from, but bit back the acid question. There was no reason to get angry at him, after all. He was only doing his job and trying to help her. But she still didn't like what he was saying.

"You need rest, Miss Collins," he continued. "Take a couple of months at least—more if you can manage it—and just rest. Catch up on your reading, lie in the sun. You need to avoid the kind of physical and emotional strain you've been under these last months." He shrugged slightly. "Vegas is full of show people, and I've seen quite a few of them professionally. I know what a performance takes out of a person. You just don't have that kind of energy."

Over the public address-system a tinny request filtered into the room. "Dr. Easton, call three-zero-one, please. Dr. Easton, call three-zero-one."

The young doctor smiled faintly. "They're playing my song." Very soberly he added, "There will be other roles, Miss Collins. Take care of yourself for them." He turned and left the room.

Tara stared at the closed door for a long time, her mind in turmoil. Yes, there would be other roles, but who knew how long she'd have to wait for one as terrific as the lead part in *Celebration!*—a big-budget film adapted from a recent best-seller and a sure bet to capture every major award next year.

Angry and resentful, Tara badly needed to lash out at something—or someone. Devlin would do. Snatching her hand from beneath his, she demanded irately, "Do you mind telling me how in hell I managed to acquire a fiancé while I was unconscious?"

Devlin folded his arms over his chest and regarded her with amusement. "Well, I see you're back to your spry and sassy self," he commented dryly.

"Answer me, dammit!"

"There's a perfectly reasonable explanation, Tara."

She didn't wait for it. In a few short, well-chosen words she told him exactly what she thought of his temperament, manners, intelligence, dubious ancestry, and general claim to humanity. She neither swore nor yelled, but her soft voice would have stripped the bark off a sapling at twenty paces.

Devlin listened with an air of great interest and ill-suppressed amusement, which maddened Tara all the more. She wanted him to yell at her, dammit, not smile with that infuriatingly calm expression. Trying to think of some way to goad him, she paused for a breath, which he took advantage of.

"Did you want the news of your collapse splashed all over the newspapers?" he asked mildly.

She had the odd feeling that the wind had been taken out of her sails. "No, of course not," she muttered. "But—"

"I had to be in a position of authority to keep the whole thing under wraps, Tara. Being your intended husband was the only idea I could come up with on the spur of the moment. But, of course, if you have a better idea . . ." He shrugged.

He sounded reasonable. He sounded so reasonable, in fact, that she was immediately suspicious.

"And just how did you account for the lack of an engagement ring *and* the fact that there's been no public announcement?" she asked nastily.

"The absence of a ring," he explained placidly, "was easy to explain. You were filming a scene at the moment of collapse, so naturally you weren't wearing your jewelry."

Tara was both baffled and disturbed. Baffled because he refused to fight with her; any one of the insults she had heaped upon his head moments before should have drawn a fire-and-brimstone response. Disturbed because she sensed he was quite pleased with himself, and *that* was enough to put any sane woman on her guard. "And the lack of an announcement?" she persisted.

"Also simple. I merely informed interested parties—meaning the chief administrator here and Dr. Easton—that we intended to keep the engagement secret for as long as possible, in order to avoid irritating questions from the press. I might add," he went on coolly, "that neither the administrator nor Easton was surprised by my request—show people being notorious for such secrecy."

"Oh." Tara was painfully aware of just how small and meek her voice sounded, and made a determined effort to strengthen it. "Well, thanks for . . . for keeping it quiet. But there's really no need to go on with it now."

"I suppose not," he answered indifferently, and for the second time since waking up Tara had to restrain herself from looking for something to throw at him. That her reaction was extremely unreasonable did not escape her, but she didn't bother to defend it or explain it—even to herself.

"Are you going to take the doctor's advice?" Devlin asked as if he didn't particularly care.

She must not have heard right when she thought he said he wanted her, she assured herself with silent fierceness. The man standing beside her bed obviously wanted nothing more than to file away this exceedingly distasteful episode into the slot marked "duty" and go on with his life. It was maddening.

Realizing that he was waiting patiently for an answer to his question, Tara murmured hastily, "Yes, of course I will." And then, bitterly, "I don't really have a choice, do I?"

Devlin strolled casually over to the window and stood looking out with a curious air of detachment. "So you'll give up your part in *Celebration!*?"

"How did you . . ." Tara stared at him as realization dawned. "My God, you're backing it!"

"I'm one of the backers," he answered easily.

"Well, I'll bet this illness of mine has made you terribly happy," she accused acidly.

"Not particularly." His voice was unruffled. "You're a fine actress, Tara, and perfect for the part. We'll have a hard time replacing you."

"Then don't!" The plea was out before Tara could stop it. "You can postpone production for a few months."

Softly, flatly, without looking at her, Devlin said, "I thought you refused to ask for favors, Tara."

"Forget it!" she snapped immediately, turning her gaze to the ceiling, hating herself for having forgotten her pride. And to ask *him* . . . him, of all people!

Ignoring her outburst, Devlin spoke in a disinterested tone, as if to himself. "I suppose it could be arranged. The projected release date isn't until next summer, and it'll take less than six months for production—"

"I said forget it! Don't do me any favors, Devlin. I don't need you. I don't need anyone!" Turning to glare at him, she caught the tail end of a keen, oddly searching look from his remarkable silver eyes. And then he was staring calmly out the window again.

"Would it make you feel any better if each of us benefited from the postponement?" he asked absently, his attention apparently focused on something outside.

Tara attempted to see his expression and found it impossible. "Benefited? What do you mean?"

"I'll postpone production for six months, giving you until the first of the year to recuperate."

"And in return?" she asked warily.

"You do me a . . . small favor."

"I knew there was a hook in it," she exploded. "If you think I'll become your mistress just for a lousy part—" Her voice broke off abruptly as she received a steely-eyed look from him, which made her feel suddenly small and uncertain.

"Wait until you're asked, Tara."

Flushing uncomfortably, she muttered, "What's the favor?" Damn, why did she always end up on the defensive with him!

"You sure you want to even hear it? Put aside your scruples and all that?" His voice was coolly mocking, his attention once more fixed on whatever was so engrossing outside the window.

For a brief moment Tara thought fondly of making a wax doll in his image and sticking pins in painful places. She pushed the pleasant image from her mind and said flatly, "The favor, Devlin. Stop playing with me."

He raised one hand, the fingers tapping softly, absently against the glass in front of him. Just when Tara was on the point of screaming at him in frustration, he finally spoke.

"It's really very simple, Tara. In return for my postponing the film, you will become my fiancée."

Chapter 3

"*Are* you out of your mind?" Tara yelped, and then, before he could respond, she went on quickly, "No, don't answer that! Insane people never admit to insanity, do they? They hold to it tooth and nail that they're just as sane as everyone else."

"Hear me out, Tara."

"Why?" she demanded angrily. "I don't like what I've heard so far."

Folding his arms across his chest, Devlin turned slightly and leaned a shoulder against the window, smiling across at her. "I'm not the devil, Tara, and I'm not asking for your soul in payment for a favor."

"Aren't you?" Longing for the strength to get up and slap his infuriatingly amused face, she spoke from between gritted teeth. "I don't want to marry you."

"I didn't ask you to marry me."

The mild comment caused her to stare at him in bewilderment. "Then just exactly what did you ask?"

"I really didn't ask anything," he pointed out in the tone of a man explaining something simple to a dimwit. "I simply said that I would postpone production of the film if you would agree to become my fiancée."

"But not to marry you?"

"That's right."

Tara wondered vaguely if her illness had left her with a sluggish mind, or if he wasn't making any sense. "You're going to have to clarify that."

"Okay, I'll put it into terms you can't possibly misunderstand." His voice was dry. "For six months you will act the part of my fiancée—if you accept the deal, of course. Needless to say, the bargain hinges on your ability to be convincing in the role."

Tara decided to let the dig at her acting ability pass. "But *why*? I mean, why do you want a fiancée? And why *me*?"

With hooded eyes and an expressionless face, Devlin murmured, "There is a certain young lady whom I wish to . . . discourage. I've found it difficult to accomplish that without seriously offending either her or her father, who happens to be rather important to me, owing to an upcoming business venture."

She looked at him warily. "I find it hard to believe, Devlin, that with all your . . . charm, you're unable to get yourself out of an entanglement."

"Did I say it was an entanglement?" He shook his head, looking faintly amused. "The young lady simply misconstrued a purely paternal interest and—"

"Paternal!" Tara's eyes widened. "How old is this young lady of yours?"

"She isn't mine," Devlin said, showing impatience for the first time. "Julie is seventeen."

"You should be ashamed of yourself," Tara scolded automatically, something inside her laughing at the idea of Devlin—strong, assured Devlin—caught in the passionate toils of a seventeen-year-old's blind infatuation.

Defending himself irritably, Devlin muttered, "I didn't do anything to encourage her, for God's sake—"

"Doesn't she think a nineteen-year age difference is important?" Tara interrupted, still tickled by his predicament.

"Not so that you'd notice." He shrugged ruefully. "Part of the blame can be laid at her father's door. Jake Holman would like nothing better than to see his daughter married to me—with the idea of welding together two financial empires, I suppose. I've tried to tell him that I'm not particularly interested in settling down at the moment, and certainly not with a girl young enough to be my daughter, but the hints just roll off his back without making the least impression."

"Poor Devlin!" Tara mocked with a grin.

He grimaced. "I thought the situation would appeal to your sadistic sense of humor."

"It does." She enjoyed his wry discomfort for a moment longer, then went on dryly, "I grant the problem, Devlin, but I really don't see that there's any urgency in solving it. All you have to do is stay away from her for a while, and it'll all blow over."

"That's just it—I can't stay away from her. Holman is worse than an eel, when it comes to being pinned down, and he won't talk business in an office, God only knows why. Anyway, my mother has invited him to spend a couple of weeks with her and my stepfather at their ranch in Texas next month. It'll be my best chance to have him in one place long enough to convince him to join me in this export deal I've worked out with a European country."

"I don't see—"

"Julie," Devlin interrupted flatly, "will be tagging along with her father. And since she has a tendency to cling like a limpet and look embarrassingly adoring, it will make a sticky situation—to say the least."

"Then don't go," Tara advised practically. "Surely you could find another time to talk to Holman about the deal."

"I probably could, although it wouldn't be easy. The man's the proverbial rolling stone. But I agreed to attend this little house party before I knew Julie was coming, and my mother would never forgive me if I backed out."

"Your mother?" She stared at him, fascinated by this completely unexpected leaning toward filial obedience. "Why is your mother so set on having you in Texas?"

"She wants me to get married."

"To Julie?"

"To Dracula's mother, if the union would produce reasonably normal grandchildren," Devlin answered wryly. "I don't think she has her eye on Julie, though. If I know Mother she'll trot out the entire female population of northern Texas."

Amused, Tara exclaimed, "But if you explained—"

Devlin shook his head. "You don't know my mother. Whoever coined the phrase 'iron hand in the velvet glove' must have been thinking of her. I shudder to think what she'd do to me if I didn't show up at her house party."

Tara tried, and failed, to picture a woman formidable enough to command the obedience of a son as strong as Devlin. The image just wouldn't form. Giving up, she said slowly, "And you expect that your arrival with a bogus fiancée will put a stop both to Julie's infatuation and your mother's matchmaking. Isn't that a little drastic—especially as far as your mother's concerned?"

He shrugged. "Not really."

She studied him carefully. "What about your mother's feelings when the fictitious engagement ends? Won't she be upset?"

"If I know Mother," he replied coolly, "she'll rake me over the coals for making a horrible mistake and try to convince me to patch things up. When that doesn't work, she'll start lining up suitable candidates again."

Tara wondered if the situation could possibly be as simple as Devlin maintained. She shook her head in bemusement. "I'll accept that for the moment, but only because I don't know your mother. But why *me*, Devlin? Surely some other woman—"

He cut her off abruptly. "I couldn't risk it with another woman. I don't mean to sound conceited,

Tara, but another woman could easily try to take advantage of a fake engagement."

Not really surprised by his cynical statement, Tara studied him thoughtfully. "And I wouldn't do that?"

"Not a chance," Devlin replied with reassuring promptness. "When it comes to dealing with other people, Tara, you're one of the most honest women I've ever met."

Tara had an uneasy feeling that he'd qualified the compliment, but she wasn't sure just how. "So you trust me not to take advantage of you."

"Completely."

It occurred to Tara then—belatedly—that it was Devlin who was taking advantage. She was ill and she wanted that part in his film badly. He was using both circumstances ruthlessly for his own gain. The realization rekindled her anger toward him. She turned slightly in the bed so that she was lying on her side facing him. "Your little plan's full of holes."

He walked over to the chair beside the bed and sat down. "Really? I thought it covered all the bases rather nicely."

Her fingers clutched the covers nervously. If only she could wipe that mocking smile off his face once and for all! "Well, you were wrong! In the first place it puts me exactly where I *don't* want to be, which is in the position of a woman using your influence to advance my career. I won't do it, Devlin."

"We'll keep the engagement secret, of course," he responded patiently. "Only my family and my mother's houseguests will know about it."

"And if there's a leak to the press?"

He shrugged. "Then we'll have a terrific fight—publicly, if you like—and simply recapture our reputation for being mortal enemies. The broken engagement will become one of Hollywood's tragic tales, and that will be that."

Against her will Tara had to admit to herself that, with the reputation the two of them had built up, the public would most likely consider the brief engagement a case of temporary insanity and dismiss it. But she still had an objection, and it was, in her opinion, a major one.

"I don't trust you, Devlin. You take what you can get with both hands and then reach for more." Her voice was even. "What about that little scene the doctor interrupted? Can I expect that sort of thing if I accept your deal?"

"Only if that's what you want, Tara," he answered casually. "I won't deny that I still want you. You're a beautiful woman and I still have memories of you lying naked in my arms."

Tara flushed with embarrassment at his blunt words and anger at her own surge of memory.

Ignoring her reaction—if he noticed it at all—Devlin went on, "but I'm sure you're fully capable of keeping me at arm's length even while pretending to be my loving fiancée."

"I certainly am," she snapped, and was immediately alarmed at how defensive she sounded even to her own ears.

His eyes narrowed slightly, a mocking glint showing in the silvery depths. " 'The lady doth protest too much, methinks,' " he quoted softly.

Tara's flush deepened, and her blue eyes sparkled angrily. Oh, damn the man! You're an actress, she told herself fiercely, so act! It wasn't exactly easy to be dignified with her face flaming, but she gave it her best shot. "I'm not protesting at all, Devlin," she managed coolly. "I'm simply stating a fact. Any relationship we had ended three years ago. This bargain of yours is just that—a deal, a business agreement."

"I see we understand each other completely." His eyes were hidden by lowered lids, his face calm. "Do I take it that you agree to the deal?"

A sneering voice inside Tara's head warned bitterly that she was making a terrible mistake by even considering Devlin's insane proposition, but she wasn't really surprised to hear the words that emerged from her mouth. "I agree. I'll pretend to be your fiancée for six months in return for your postponing *Celebration!*" For the first time, she wondered why he had asked for six months even though he only needed her for a couple of weeks. But before she could ask the question, Devlin was speaking briskly.

"That's settled, then. The doctors want you to remain here until the end of the week. I have to fly out to New York about then, so I'll settle you in Jim's apartment, where you can spend a couple of weeks lying in the sun and recovering your strength."

"That's not necessary," she objected immediately. "I can go home to recover."

Devlin lifted a skeptical eyebrow. "And run the gauntlet of L.A. reporters?" he asked. "Do you really think you'll be up to that, Tara?"

She frowned at him, undecided.

Sighing, he said patiently, "I won't be around, Tara, if that's what you're worrying about. I'll be in

New York for at least two weeks, possibly longer. What would be the point of your flying to L.A. only to get on another plane two weeks later? You can rest just as easily here. Better, in fact, because the press thinks you left with the production crew."

"And when you come back?"

"Then we'll catch a plane to Texas."

She stared at him a moment longer, then shrugged, feeling suddenly very weary. "All right."

He nodded and rose to his feet, smiling. "I'd better leave you alone to get some rest. I think you've been through enough for one day."

"You can say that again," she muttered.

Not rising to the bait, Devlin went toward the door, then hesitated and gave her a thoughtful look. "I do have one question, Tara."

"You can ask. I don't promise to answer."

In a very neutral voice, he asked, "Has there been anyone since me?"

"Loads. I'm a popular lady."

"Don't be flippant, Tara."

She had an absurd desire to burst into tears. "You have no right to ask me that question," she said tightly.

"I was the first man in your bed, Tara. That gives me the right." It might have been her imagination, but she thought his voice was slightly strained. Holding onto that thought, she made her own voice indifferent.

"That and ten cents will get you a dime."

For a moment his lean face had a masklike look that was oddly disturbing. Then he was smiling wryly. "That's my Tara," he murmured. "Stubborn to the end." Without another word he opened the door and left the room.

Tara stared at the closed door for a long moment, trying to rid herself of the sudden notion that every move made in this room during the past hour had been carefully planned in advance, like a game of chess. And she had been the pawn . . .

A sudden crash of thunder rumbled outside, and Tara started, pulling the covers up around her neck with a faint moan. Oh, no—a storm! For as long as she could remember, she had been terrified of them. That would really put the finishing touches on an awful day. She only hoped Devlin wouldn't come back and find her cowering beneath the covers like a frightened child. Some actress she was!

Tara pulled her sunglasses down her nose and blinked in the bright light, her attention caught by the rainbow glitter of the diamond ring on the third finger of her left hand. She stared absently down at the ring.

It had been on her finger for nearly two weeks, ever since Devlin had left for New York, and she still felt odd whenever she looked at it. She had told herself time and again that the feeling was caused simply by the fact that she didn't want to wear *his* ring, but part of her found a different cause, one she didn't want to accept.

The ring, part of her insisted, was a fantasy, an illusion. It was no more real than the props she used in films, something to be worn for a brief time and then put away. Make-believe. A phantom symbol of ancient origin, meant to convey love and possession and the bonding of two lives.

It was a mirage, because it wasn't really hers.

Dropping her sunglasses onto a small table by the chaise longue, Tara concentrated on the sparkling ring. The stone was oval, the setting very old and delicate, like cobwebs spun of fine gold. It even looked unreal, she told herself silently, and then abruptly remembered what Devlin had said when he had tossed the tiny box into her lap as they were driving away from the hospital.

"Here's the main prop for your role. Wear it in good health."

He hadn't even asked her if she liked it.

The doorbell chimed suddenly, jerking Tara out of her depressed thoughts. She turned to look over her shoulder and came nose to nose with Ah Poo, who had jumped silently up on the table at her side. Momentarily forgetting the unexpected visitor, she smiled faintly, and murmured, "Hello, cat. Come to cheer me up?"

Ah Poo blinked at her, and when she felt her eyes beginning to cross like his, she drew back and blinked too. "Drat you, cat. Don't stare like that. I'll end up staring at my own nose permanently."

She rose to her feet and flexed her shoulders experimentally, waiting for the telltale prickle that would warn her she'd spent too much time on the balcony. It didn't come. She passed a satisfied hand over her flat stomach, pleased with the contrast between her smooth golden flesh and the bright-yellow bikini. Luckily for Tara, she was that exceedingly rare bird—a redhead who tanned instead of freckled. Thanks to her hours in the sun, she had completely lost her hospital pallor. That, along with the uninterrupted rest and Mrs. Henson's talent for cooking, had made her feel almost as good as new.

"Prroopp!" Ah Poo's loud approval was echoed almost immediately by a hushed and appreciative masculine voice coming from the open glass doors. "I couldn't agree with you more, Mr. Cat. She is a definite addition to my balcony."

Remembering the ringing doorbell, Tara swung around in surprise to confront a total stranger.

He was about her own height, with sun-lightened brown hair and a tanned face that looked as though it wore a cheerful smile most of the time. Warm brown eyes swept over her slender body in a thoroughly male appraisal and crinkled in apology for his familiarity.

"An early Christmas present?" he inquired hopefully. "A late birthday present?"

Coming rapidly to the conclusion that she was facing her formerly absent host, Tara relaxed and smiled in amusement. "I'm afraid not," she said with a slight wave of her left hand. The engagement ring caught the light and turned it to brilliant color.

The man's face fell in dramatic disappointment. "Oh, no! Someone's already caught you, the lucky so-and-so." He staggered forward and dropped into the lounge chair, returning Ah Poo's stare.

Interrupting the dueling match of feline and human eyes, Tara said with a laugh, "I do hope you're Jim Thomas."

"Fair lady, I've never answered to anything but Jim in my life . . . but you may call me anything you like." He cocked an intelligent brow at her. "And you are Tara Collins, unless there's a wedding band next to that disgusting rock."

She grinned. "Not yet."

"Devlin, eh?" He smiled crookedly.

She nodded and ventured hesitantly, "He told you about us?"

"Not a word," Jim replied with a shrug. "But since I expected Devlin here and found you instead, and since you're wearing a ring that I happen to recognize as belonging to Dev's family, *and* since Mrs. Henson informed me that Mr. Bradley's fiancée was on the balcony, I just naturally assumed . . ."

Tara smiled in spite of herself and tried to think of some way to explain her engagement, to a man who was obviously a close friend of Devlin's. But before she could gather her thoughts, he went on conversationally, "Funny thing about this engagement of yours and Dev's." He linked his hands across his trim abdomen and ignored Ah Poo's mutters of dislike with supreme indifference. "I talked to Dev less than a month ago, and I could swear he wasn't thinking along the lines of matrimony. And I distinctly remember reading somewhere that there's been a running feud between you two for years."

"Things change," Tara offered lamely.

"Obviously." He grinned at her discomfort. "Don't worry, I won't pester you with questions. I'll just assume that love conquered all and leave it at that."

Wanting desperately to change the subject, Tara said easily, "Devlin said you'd be in Europe for the summer, but since you're home now, I'll be glad to get a hotel room."

"Nonsense!" Jim cut her off promptly. "You'll stay here as long as you like. This place does have an extra bedroom, you know." His grin was both friendly and charming. "I'm sure Dev won't mind. After all, if a man can't trust his fiancée and his best friend, who can he trust?"

"Well, if you're sure you don't mind . . ." Tara wasn't particularly concerned with Devlin's opinion of the matter. He had no control over her life.

"Of course I don't mind. As a matter of fact it'll be nice just to be able to carry on a conversation with someone who speaks English. I made the mistake of going to Paris and trying to struggle through with basic French. The results were disastrous."

Eyeing him with curiosity, Tara pulled forward a deck chair and sank into it. "You don't exactly sound like the typical tourist," she observed. "Was it a business trip?"

"Unofficially. Devlin had already laid the groundwork for an export deal, and I went over to cement the ties of friendly relations." He smiled modestly. "You may have noticed that Dev's a bit . . . overpowering sometimes. Especially in business matters. I usually wind up being his goodwill ambassador."

Tara was puzzled by the relationship. "You mean you . . . work with Devlin?"

"Dev would probably object strongly to the term 'work,' " Jim told her wryly. "He's taken a great deal of delight in telling me for nearly twenty years that I'm a good-for-nothing lazy soul. We met in college, and I've been more or less tagging along behind him ever since. I had enough sense to invest in some of his earlier ventures, and since they were successful, I'm quite happy to help him out whenever I can." He calmly removed Ah Poo's flexing paw from his arm and went on without the slightest change in tone. "Your cat doesn't like me."

Tara had the feeling Jim had deliberately understated his importance in Devlin's business affairs, but she had no intention of prying. Frowning a warning at her cat, she said sternly, "Behave yourself!" and then looked apologetically at her host. "I'm sorry. I'm afraid Ah Poo isn't terribly impressed with the majority of mankind."

"Ah Poo?" Jim stared at the glaring animal. "Well, I must admit the name suits you, cat, although I don't know exactly why."

"Devlin named him when he was a kitten." Immediately Tara could have bitten her tongue. *Damn* Devlin for getting her in the middle of this fake engagement and then leaving her to sink or swim! What if Jim asked why a cat that was obviously at least a couple of years old should have been named by her fiancé, who was supposed to have been Tara's worst enemy at the time?

But he didn't. Tactfully ignoring her flushed face, he said calmly, "That sounds like something Dev would do. I'll bet Ah Poo thinks Dev's the next best thing to tuna, too."

"He adores him," Tara managed weakly.

"I knew it." Holding up a finger for emphasis, Jim said in a warning tone to the cat, "You are a guest in my home, Ah Poo, and you had better remember that. I also happen to be Devlin's best friend—human friend, that is—so remember *that*. If you're nice to me, I might even be persuaded to buy you some tuna. Or liver."

Crossed china-blue eyes regarded Jim for a long, unblinking minute, and then the cat stepped delicately onto his lap. Settling down comfortably, he began to purr.

"Hey!" Jim looked astonished. "He understood me!"

"I hate to burst your bubble," Tara said, amused, "but I'm afraid it's strictly cupboard love. You offered liver, which is a particular favorite of his."

"Oh." Jim stared down at the cat. "Toady!" he accused.

The phone rang just then, and Jim hastily picked up the cat and set him down gently beside the chaise. "I'll bet that's Dev," he exclaimed. "Let me answer it, Tara. I want to have a little fun."

Tara nodded in bemusement, wondering just what kind of fun he had in mind. She didn't really think Devlin was on the phone, since she hadn't heard a word from him once he'd left for New York. But maybe he was calling to say he'd be late or early . . . or whatever.

Curious in spite of herself, she rose, put on her thigh-length terry wrap, and followed Jim into the apartment. He was speaking cheerfully into the receiver.

"Hi, there, old man, how's life treating you these days?" He smiled wickedly at Tara as she perched on the arm of the couch and listened in amusement. It must be Devlin after all. "What's that?" Jim continued. "Well, of course it's me. Who else should answer the phone in my apartment? Who? Sure, she's here. As a matter of fact I was just going to treat her to a night on the town." He grimaced and held the receiver abruptly away from his ear. "Sure," he added hastily, "sure, you can talk to her." With one hand over the mouthpiece he extended the phone to Tara. "My, but he's touchy. He wants to talk to you."

She accepted the phone, wondering absently why Devlin should be touchy. He certainly wasn't jealous! Mindful of her role in this farce, and of Jim's unabashed eavesdropping, she spoke softly into the receiver. "Hello, darling."

After a moment of silence Devlin said dryly, "I take it Jim doesn't know the truth about our engagement."

"I miss you too, darling," Tara purred, trying desperately to convince herself that she was simply acting a part.

"He's in the room?"

"Yes . . . that's right."

Devlin chuckled. "I'm looking forward to watching you play the loving fiancée, Tara. From the sound of it you do it very well. Will I get a welcome home kiss too?"

Knowing Devlin would catch her meaning, she made her voice as seductive as possible. "You'll get exactly what's coming to you," she murmured, and then smiled for Jim's benefit.

Devlin laughed again. "Just don't have a knife handy, okay?" Before she could respond, he went on, "I just called to tell you I'll be back sometime tomorrow afternoon."

"I'll look forward to it."

Softly, he added, "Tell me you love me, Tara."

She was immediately furious with his underhanded tactics. Nevertheless she was obliged to bite back her anger, because of Jim. Injecting a light, teasing note into her voice, she said, "That's not fair, darling."

"Backing out of the deal already, Tara? It hinged, if you'll remember, on your ability to be convincing." When she remained stubbornly silent, he added smoothly, "Jim will expect it."

She gripped the receiver until her knuckles turned white, but her expression remained tender—a credit to her acting abilities, although Devlin, on the other end of the line, was unable to appreciate it. Vowing with silent wrath to get even with Devlin Bradley before she was much older, she said adoringly, "I love you."

There was a long silence, and Tara could have sworn she heard him catch his breath. Then he was saying calmly, "I could easily become addicted to the sound of that. I'll see you tomorrow, honey. Put Jim on, will you?"

Tara handed the receiver to Jim and fled immediately to her bedroom. She was very much afraid she was going to burst into tears of sheer frustration and rage, and she didn't want her host to witness it. She wanted to break things, to scream at Devlin for being the sadistic beast that he was.

He had done it deliberately, damn him. Deliberately. Oh, why hadn't she realized just what this ridiculous masquerade would mean? She would have to gaze at him adoringly whenever they were together, pretend to be in love with him. And he'd probably demand over and over again that she vow her love in front of everyone.

Fuming, she changed quickly from her bikini into a pair of slacks and a peach-colored blouse. Slipping her feet into a pair of house shoes, she brushed her hair quickly and headed back toward the living room. She wouldn't cry. She wouldn't *let* herself cry.

Jim had just hung up the phone when she returned. He turned to face her with a concerned frown. "Why didn't you tell me you were convalescing?" he demanded.

Tara sank down on one end of the couch and smiled wryly. "I've known you exactly half an hour. When did I have time to tell you? Besides, it's not anything serious."

"Exhaustion isn't serious?" He grunted in sardonic amusement. "No wonder Dev nearly took my head off when I repeated my little remark about taking you out on the town."

Her blue eyes sparkled with anger. "He told you not to take me anywhere?"

He wandered toward the bar in the corner of the room and reached for a decanter. "Something like that," he murmured.

Frowning, Tara watched her fingers tap out an irritated tattoo on the arm of the couch. "I think I *would* like to go somewhere tonight," she remarked in an innocent voice. "Take in a show, maybe."

Jim turned to her, laughing. "I have to admit Dev knows you well." He chuckled. "He warned me you'd say something like that."

"Like what?" Her mouth turned sulky, and she was immediately annoyed with herself for making the childish gesture.

"Like that you suddenly felt like going out tonight. He said he would have told you not to go out, but that he knew you'd do it anyway, just to spite him. So he told me instead."

Tara looked at him speculatively. "There's a new comic playing just down the street," she mentioned in an offhand manner. "It isn't very far, and Devlin wouldn't have to know . . ."

Jim was shaking his head. "I've got my orders."

"Coward," she muttered.

"You're so right. Devlin's a hell of a lot bigger than I am, you know. I try not to irritate him any more than necessary." His voice was threaded with amusement.

Tara studied her nails thoughtfully. "I don't need an escort, you know. I can go by myself."

"Sorry, Tara. You're under house arrest, I'm afraid." Jim shook his head ruefully. "Devlin sure has you pegged. He told me my innocent little joke would have you hell-bent to go out. He also told me to keep you here even if I had to lock you in your room."

"That's barbaric!" she snapped, momentarily forgetting her role. "Devlin Bradley can't control my life from a distance of two thousand miles. If he thinks I'm going to—" She broke off abruptly to stare with impotent fury at Jim's amused face.

"Drink, Tara?" he asked mildly, holding up a decanter.

"White wine, please," she murmured, deciding that she needed a drink. But what she really needed was to have Devlin's neck within reach of her itching fingers.

Jim crossed the room to hand her a glass, then sank down on the other end of the couch with his own drink. "Devlin told me to remind you—in case you were thinking of climbing out your bedroom window—that it's twelve stories down."

Tara glared at him from beneath her lashes. "Funny," she muttered. "That's very funny."

Jim chuckled softly. "I'll bet you plan to have the word 'obey' taken out of the marriage vows."

Suddenly Tara saw the humor in the situation and laughed. "Do you really think Devlin would let me?" she asked.

Jim grinned. "No. But I'll tell you what I think *would* happen. I think you'd slip the minister twenty bucks to leave out the 'obey,' and then Dev would slip him fifty to leave it in."

Tara sighed ruefully. "He does seem to have the irritating ability to read my mind."

"At least you won't be able to say that your husband doesn't understand you," he remarked cheerfully. "I think you two are going to have a terrific marriage."

Tara sipped her wine hastily as she suddenly remembered that she and Devlin weren't really going to be married. For some inexplicable reason that thought made her feel very depressed. Unwilling to either analyze or face her emotions, she asked quickly, "Did Dev tell you he'd be back tomorrow?"

Jim nodded. "We're not to meet him at the airport, though." He paused, and his brown eyes were curious. "How did you two meet, anyway—or is that a nosy question?"

"Not at all." She smiled at him, glad for the slight change of topic. "We met at a premiere party for a film he backed."

"And it was love at first sight?"

Tara grinned in spite of herself. "Not quite. To be perfectly truthful, I didn't want to have anything to do with him. Have you heard the expression 'casting couch'? "

A gleam of understanding shone in Jim's eyes. "Of course. And I've heard it used in connection with some of Dev's films. I never believed it, though."

"Neither do I—now. But at the time, I'd heard of several actresses who had gotten parts solely because of their association with Devlin. It wasn't really his doing. It's just that producers and directors tended to hire women Devlin was interested in, to . . . court his favor, so to speak."

"And you didn't like that?"

Tara shook her head. "I wanted to be cast for my ability, not my relationships with anyone in the industry. So I decided that the safest way to avoid any prejudice would be to avoid Devlin."

"Did he lay siege to you?" Jim asked with a grin.

"Something like that," she murmured, remembering the two weeks after she had met Devlin. Each day a huge basket of roses had arrived at her apartment, accompanied by a card with a phone number and a single-word question—"Please?" Finally, hip-deep in roses of every color, and sympathetic to the plight of the delivery boy, Tara had finally given in and called Devlin.

She looked up to encounter Jim's gaze and went on lightly, "We started seeing each other. Quietly. I was still determined not to be accused of trying to find an easy way into films."

"The secrecy must have been hard on the two of you," Jim offered quietly.

Tara nodded slowly, staring down at her glass. It had not only been hard, she thought, but also had led to a degree of intimacy she had not been prepared for. "Devlin didn't like 'sneaking around,' as he put it," she murmured, almost to herself. "I wasn't happy about it myself. There were . . . disagreements."

Painfully she remembered the argument that had caused their final break-up. The casting director had promised her a part in one of Devlin's films, but at the last minute she had discovered that Devlin had recommended another actress for the role. Hurt and angry, Tara had lashed out at him. Instead of taking her seriously, he had asked her to quit acting and become his wife. She had refused. Emphatically.

"Tara?"

She shook the memories away and smiled brightly. "Everything worked out all right, though," she told Jim.

"Obviously." He smiled.

Tara returned the smile, but her thoughts were on the public fights and the private misery of the past three years. She had still been attracted to Devlin after they had parted, and the only way to fight that attraction had been to fight him. After the blow to his pride her rejection had brought, Devlin had been more than willing to fight with her.

Now she watched Jim get up to refill their glasses and wondered vaguely, but not for the first time, what had happened between Devlin and the blond model he was supposed to have been so seriously involved with. The press had certainly indicated that marriage was imminent. What had happened between them? Did Jim know?

But it didn't matter. Tara wasn't interested in that other woman. Not at all.

Chapter 4

"How do you like the ring?" Jim asked as he handed Tara her glass and sank down on the couch.

Roused from her thoughts, Tara looked down at the glittering diamond and then at her host. "It's beautiful." She tilted her head to one side, curious in spite of herself. "You mentioned a while ago that you recognized the ring. Is there something special about it that I don't know?"

"Well, it has a curse," Jim confided with a grin.

"A what?" She stared at him blankly.

Chanting as though casting a spell, Jim recited, "As long as the ring is passed from eldest son to eldest son, and given with true love to the wives of their choice, the Bradley clan will always have good luck. But if ever an eldest son gives the ring without first giving his heart, bad luck will befall the entire clan."

Tara thought that over for a minute. "You're pulling my leg—right?" she asked wryly.

"Not at all." Jim chuckled softly. "I'm surprised Dev hasn't told you. The curse originated sometime in the seventeenth century. One stormy night an eldest son performed a daring act of heroism and rescued a beautiful—and wealthy—maiden. She rewarded him with the ring and her heart."

"And the curse?" Tara asked.

"An old gypsy was responsible for that, a little later on. A Bradley ancestor took the ring to be blessed and ended up with a blessing—or a curse—depending on your point of view, I suppose. Anyway, it's been a fairly consistent curse. As long as an eldest son gave the ring with love, the whole family prospered."

Tara was fascinated. "What if he gave the ring for a reason other than love?"

Jim grimaced. "Bad luck. It happened several times down through the years. Dev's grandfather, for instance, sold the ring after his first wife died. He had remarried by then—for money, not love—and then decided that he needed capital for investments. So he and his second wife decided to sell the ring. His timing was rotten. The stock market collapsed two days later. Ruined him completely."

Tara stared down at the ring. "But . . . the ring . . ."

"Oh, you have the original ring," Jim confirmed. "It turned out that Dev's grandmother had the ring copied and hid the original. It turned up again in an old trunk, just a few years ago."

Tara watched absently as Ah Poo leaped up between them on the couch. "I've heard of stories like that," she said, "but I certainly never expected to land right in the middle of a family curse."

Jim laughed. "Well, you certainly don't have to worry. It's obvious that Dev loves you."

Tara stared down at her empty glass for a moment, then leaned forward to place it on the coffee table. Her face was calm, but her thoughts were troubled. No, Devlin didn't love her. He trusted her. He trusted her not to take advantage of a fake engagement. He trusted her with an old and very valuable family heirloom. But he had never trusted her with his secret thoughts, his hopes and ambitions. Though he had spoken to her of his mother's hopes regarding a marriage for him, she had no idea whether he wanted to share his life with someone.

Their former relationship had been based largely on physical attraction, and their rare time together had not allowed for tender confidences and whispered dreams. The passion between them had been fiery and primitive, sweeping all before it in a hungry, turbulent current of sheer need. And even in that moment of ultimate arousal, that eternity of drowning pleasure in which two separate people melded into a single entity, each had held something back. Tara because of some nameless private fear that she herself didn't understand, and Devlin . . .

Devlin. He had been tender and passionate, gentle and demanding—everything a young woman could want and need from that all-important first lover. He had never hurt her, never disappointed her. He had taken her to the heights of ecstasy time after time, each soaring flight more wondrous than the last. And always some sixth sense—or perhaps it was only the intuition that women have possessed down through the ages—had warned her that he was holding back something of himself.

She didn't know what that "something" was.

Tara came back to the present, to hear Jim say cheerfully, "Now that we have that little matter settled, I'm going to ask Mrs. Henson what we're having for dinner. And then how about a fast game of strip poker?"

Tara managed a faint smile. "How about an equally fast game of gin rummy?" she countered dryly.

"Spoilsport!" he grumbled in a voice of mock disgust, and then grinned and headed for the kitchen.

Alone but for Ah Poo's silent presence, Tara stared down at the ring on her hand until the glowing diamond seemed to have imprinted itself on her brain. So much history, she thought vaguely, so much of human passions and greed had accompanied this polished gem throughout its four-hundred-year life span. And how much influence had the brilliant stone actually exerted on those events?

Not much, probably. When a man married for the wrong reasons he was asking for trouble. And people were always suffering unexplained deaths and accidents. Fortunes were won and lost, sometimes only on the roll of the dice or the turn of a card. There was nothing unusual in this history, this ring. The curse of an old gypsy was just a fable.

Ah Poo butted his head gently against Tara's arm, and she reached out to scratch him beneath the chin. Staring into his blissful blue eyes, she murmured, "I'm not superstitious, cat." And then, almost in the same breath, she added, "But your beloved Devlin's taking an awful chance."

* * *

Midway through the following afternoon Jim managed to unearth a Monopoly game, and he and Tara spent an uproarious hour winning and losing fantastic sums and arguing fiercely over who owned what, where. After landing in jail for the sixth time and realizing, to his dismay, that he was nearly broke, Jim was in the process of trying to wheedle a loan from Tara when he was suddenly distracted by Ah Poo's abrupt activity.

The cat, who had been lying on the coffee table beside the game board and interestedly watching the proceedings, leaped up suddenly and stalked over to the front door. He planted himself firmly about three feet from the portal and stared at it intently, his tail moving restlessly.

Jim lifted an eyebrow and looked quizzically at Tara. "Does he want to go out?"

Tara shook her head, trying to ignore the way her heart had suddenly begun to pound. "No. Devlin's back." She was pleased that her voice emerged casual and steady.

"He *knows* Devlin's back?" Jim asked with a blank look.

She nodded vaguely, staring toward the cat. She remembered too well that, even as a kitten, Ah Poo had always displayed an uncanny ability to know when his adored Devlin was nearby. Struggling to keep her voice under control, she murmured, "He's probably at the elevator right now."

Jim glanced down at his watch and muttered, "Then he'll be at the door about . . ." At that exact moment, a key grated in the lock.

Jim's expression of astonishment made Tara want

to giggle, but since she was dimly aware that her voice would be brittle with strain and tension, she managed to bite it back.

Devlin appeared in the open door a moment later. He barely had time to set his briefcase and larger suitcase down on the floor before Ah Poo launched himself with a howl that sounded like the battle cry of a kamikaze pilot. Jim jumped to his feet, but the alarm on his face melted into laughter as he recognized the feline delight of Ah Poo's exuberant greeting.

Tara remained where she was, seated on the floor between the couch and the coffee table, every nerve in her body throbbing with a sudden, agonizing awareness. She watched, mesmerized, as Devlin's hard features softened as he looked down at the adoring cat in his arms.

Shock ripped its way through Tara's mind with the force of a lightning bolt. She knew now why she had accepted Devlin's insane proposition, why she had gone out of her way to be hostile to him during the past three years. She knew now why she looked at other men with a disinterest she could not explain, why she had worked herself almost to death during those years just so she could sleep, and sleep without dreaming. She knew now why his presence, his touch, his voice could reassure her and excite her and anger her.

She loved him. She had loved him from the very beginning. And she had to get through the next few weeks—no, *months*—acting the part of a loving fiancée, when she wanted to be the real thing. A loving fiancée. A *loved* fiancée.

A deeply rooted instinct of self-preservation rather than acting ability kept Tara's face expressionless and her eyes wide and blank. She watched Devlin cross the room to shake hands with Jim. She met Devlin's stormy gray eyes as he looked down at her. It took only a moment to identify mockery in the luminous depths.

"Hi, sweetheart. Don't I get a kiss?"

Tara felt no anger at his underhanded tactics. She was overwhelmed by sheer panic. *He'll know!* her mind kept repeating over and over again. A temporary solution popped into her mind suddenly, and she dropped her gaze to the stacks of play money on the coffee table in front of her. In a casual voice she told him, "I'm mad at you. You told Jim not to take me anywhere."

Devlin lifted a brow and glanced at Jim, who was trying to hide a grin. Then he gently set Ah Poo down on the game board and stepped around the coffee table to grasp Tara by the upper arms. "If you won't give me a kiss, I'll take one," he said calmly, pulling her effortlessly to her feet.

His hands held her firmly, as if he half expected her to try to get away. But Tara made no move to escape him. *You're an actress,* she told herself with desperate calm. But it wasn't the actress in her who lifted her arms to encircle his neck. It was the woman in her . . . the woman who wanted to touch the man she loved.

A flicker of satisfaction showed briefly in the stormy eyes. His hands slid around to her back as he bent his dark head to take her lips. It was not a light "welcome home" kiss, and Devlin didn't try to disguise it as such. The hot demand of his lips tore through her hastily erected barriers and stirred the embers buried deep inside her to a white-hot blaze. She was powerless to fight him.

Her lips parted. Her body, guided only partly by the hand at the small of her back, molded itself against him. She felt his hands on her back burning through the thin silk of her blouse, felt his belt buckle digging into her middle with a certain painful pleasure. A hot, familiar ache began to grow in her loins.

And then she dimly heard Jim's voice, filled with laughter. "Is this an X-rated movie or can anybody watch?"

Devlin lifted his head long enough to glance over his shoulder and call his friend a very rude name that amused Jim considerably.

Tara took the opportunity to slip from Devlin's embrace and resume her former position on the floor. She moved with a grace that concealed the fact that her knees would no longer hold her up. With iron control, she said calmly, "Shall we start another game or are you two going to talk business?" She looked up to see Devlin removing his jacket and loosening his tie.

"Deal me in," he told her cheerfully, tossing the jacket onto the couch.

"We aren't playing poker," she snapped, annoyed by his utter calm. Apparently the kiss hadn't affected him in the least, though her heart was still thundering in her ears.

With a grace unusual in so large a man, Devlin dropped down on the carpet at the narrow end of the coffee table and removed Ah Poo from the game board. Ignoring Tara's comment he glanced up at Jim and said, "We can discuss business after dinner tonight. Right now I want to take all your money."

Jim took his former position across from Tara. "You'll probably take mine," he said, "but look out for Tara. She wiped me out a few minutes ago."

"Oh, I know all about how Tara plays games. Don't I, honey?"

Tara was busily clearing the board. "You should, darling," she said with false sweetness. She had no idea how she was managing to keep her voice light and even, or why her hands were steady. She was painfully aware of Devlin's nearness, of the tangy scent of his aftershave.

Silently readying the board for another game, she listened to Devlin talking casually to Jim, the actual words passing over her but the deep voice shivering along her nerve endings like an arrow across a taut bowstring. Good heavens, why hadn't she realized she loved him long before? How could she have accepted her thin disguise of hostility as truth all this time? The very fact of her reluctance to face her own feelings should have told her something long ago.

Well, she had faced the truth now. She loved him. And she couldn't tell him, because anything he might have once felt for her had been killed by her own words and actions three years ago. He hadn't loved her then, she thought sadly, but he had cared enough to ask her to be his wife. And she had rejected him angrily, bitterly, because he had meddled in the career she had worked so hard to build.

Liberation, she thought wryly. She was a member of the liberated generation, which meant that she had to prove her ability to take care of herself. How often had her mother pounded that idea into her head? How often had she lain awake at night on her narrow, uncomfortable cot and listened to her mother crying in bitter anguish over the impossibility of leaving the man she had dropped out of school to marry?

Hastily, fiercely, Tara slammed the lid down on these painful memories, which had not raised their ugly heads, except in nightmares, for sixteen years. She couldn't reopen those old wounds, not yet. Perhaps . . . perhaps not ever.

Emerging from her thoughts, Tara found to her surprise that the game had begun. She had been playing automatically. At the same moment she became aware of Devlin's voice.

"So if you don't mind, Jim, we'll stay here tonight and then start for Texas in the morning," he was saying.

"You know I don't mind," Jim responded easily.

Reaching to pick up the dice for her turn, Tara glanced warily at her bogus fiancé. "We aren't leaving until morning?" she asked.

"No reason to." Devlin reached down to scratch Ah Poo behind one ear as the cat purred contentedly in his lap. "Mother isn't expecting us for a couple of days yet." His eyes gleamed with a mischief she couldn't fathom for a moment, and then, just as she rolled the dice, the answer came.

She stared blindly down at the dice, dimly hearing Jim's voice exclaim with a laugh, "Hey, that puts you in jail!"

"It certainly does," she muttered, woodenly moving her game piece to the corner of the board. Her silent dismay had nothing to do with her bad luck in the game, but rather with Devlin's decision—deliberate, she knew—to stay the night. Jim's apartment had two bedrooms, and she knew very well that Devlin would not offer to sleep on the couch.

What had he said in the hospital? That he still wanted her but that surely she could hold him at arm's length. A week ago, even a few days ago, she had been certain of her ability to do just that. But if he took her in his arms now, she would be lost. Her love made her vulnerable, and her helpless desire for his possession left her no defense.

"By the way, Tara, what happened to Churchill?"

Devlin's casual question made her blink, and she tried to force herself to think clearly. "Oh . . . well, I know you said your mother wouldn't mind pets, but I thought that taking Churchill might be stretching things a bit. A little boy down the hall wanted a pet, and his mother didn't mind." She shrugged.

Devlin's silvery eyes warmed with amusement. "That was nice of you. I'm not saying Mother would have been upset, but she isn't terribly fond of mice."

"Mice? Churchill? What are you two talking about?" Jim looked from one to the other.

Devlin explained the story of Ah Poo, Churchill, and the padlocked cage, eliciting a roar of laughter from Jim. When his friend had finally calmed down, Devlin turned to Tara with a smile. "I'll bet Ah Poo sulked while I was gone," he remarked.

In spite of her confused emotions, she felt a smile tug at the corners of her mouth. "For three days."

Devlin's silvery eyes dropped fleetingly to her mouth, warm and caressing, and her fingers twined together nervously under the table. He was a natural actor! She could almost believe he was in love with her. No other man had ever looked at her in quite that way, she realized. It gave her a strange feeling to have him gaze at her as though she were everything he had ever wanted out of life. Strange . . . and oddly, alarmingly pleasing.

Wistfully, she allowed her eyes to follow the movements of his strong brown hands as he took his turn and rolled the dice. Looking up, she found Jim's smiling gaze on, first, Devlin and then herself. He had been completely fooled. It was there, in his eyes. He was genuinely pleased that his friend had fallen in love at last.

Tara felt sick as dismay swept over her. How many people would they hurt with this false engagement?

"Tara? It's your turn."

She reached out hastily to pick up the dice, avoiding Devlin's eyes. Why . . . oh, why hadn't she considered the pitfalls of this ridiculous situation more carefully?

"Is anything wrong, honey? You don't seem to have your mind on the game." Devlin's voice was concerned, but Tara caught the note of mockery meant for her ears alone.

"Nothing's wrong," she murmured, moving her game piece automatically on the board and wondering rather grimly how she could bear listening to the sweet endearments that fell almost constantly from Devlin's lips. She had always hated the sort of honeyed talk used carelessly in show-business circles, knowing that it was as meaningless as it was popular. She had never responded in kind to those empty endearments, but she had learned not to become angered by them.

But the same words she had accepted indifferently from other men aroused a bitter fury in her when they came from Devlin. She wasn't certain why. Perhaps because it seemed out of character for him to use such words and phrases. Or perhaps because he had never done so before. Not even three years before . . .

With a supreme effort of will Tara managed to keep her mind on the game, pushing her disturbed thoughts and emotions into a darkened corner and firmly slamming a door on them. It was a trick she had learned long ago, useful whenever she had been faced with a difficult part, and she was grateful for the ability now.

Throughout the afternoon she was able to maintain the charade of a loving fiancée. She talked easily and casually to the two men, even managing not to stiffen when Devlin put an arm around her to lead her into dinner that evening.

She fell silent during the meal, listening as Devlin and Jim talked business. Although she knew Devlin was an excellent businessman, she was nevertheless impressed by this new evidence of his obvious ability. He spoke clearly and concisely to Jim of his plans regarding the European deal, explaining exactly what he hoped to accomplish by talking to Jake Holman in Texas. Only then did Tara realize why Holman was so important. His shipping business was vital if Devlin's plans were to be successful. She mused over that fact until her attention was caught by something Jim was saying.

" . . . and Allen Stewart was very interested in your plans to form a production company of your own, Dev. He told me his London studio would be available if you needed it for a film, and that he knows several terrific technicians who'd be delighted to work with you. He even offered to subsidize the project, knowing, of course, that you've proven your ability to back winners."

Before Devlin could respond, Tara asked quietly, "Are you really planning to form your own production company?"

He looked at her with an unreadable expression, his silver eyes curiously guarded, and then shrugged. "It was just a thought. I haven't really decided," he told her casually.

"It could become a family business," Jim said cheerfully. "Dev could produce and you could star, Tara." Without knowing it, he had put his foot right in the middle of a major dispute.

"Oh, no," Tara said lightly. "I've worked with Devlin before. He's a harsh taskmaster. I shudder to think what he'd be like after we were married." Jim only laughed, but Devlin's glance made Tara feel uneasy.

Deciding abruptly that discretion was indeed the better part of valor, she rose to her feet, waving the men back when they would have risen also. "I think I'll make it an early night," she said. "I'll read for a while. If you gentlemen will excuse me, I'll leave you to your business talk." Barely waiting for their murmured acceptance and resolutely avoiding Devlin's faintly mocking gaze, she left the room.

Alone in her bedroom, Tara considered several unsettling facts, the most important one being that within the next few hours she and Devlin would be sharing this room . . . and this bed. As if drawn by a magnet, her eyes moved to the wide bed, which had seemed huge to her for two weeks and now suddenly seemed small.

Tearing her eyes from the hypnotic sight of a bed that appeared to be shrinking moment by moment, she looked at her nightgown, lying over a chair in the corner, and abruptly faced the second unsettling fact—her only nightgown was really just a few scraps of lace and satin that practically screamed a message of seduction. Ice-blue and nearly see-through, it barely reached the tops of her thighs. The matching panties only aggravated matters.

Tara wondered if Devlin had planned all this long ago. With his usual high-handedness, he had sent her motor home ahead to his mother's ranch— why, she couldn't fathom—and only informed her of the deed after the fact. Since he chose to tell her right after tossing an engagement ring in her lap, she hadn't been thinking clearly enough to question his motives. She had made an irritated remark to the effect that he might have asked her, and then had let the matter drop.

Devlin had also packed her suitcase for her. Not until after he'd left for New York did she discover that practically every sexy item of clothing she owned was in the case.

Tara liked nice things. She enjoyed the feel of silk or satin against her skin and, luckily, had the money to indulge her tastes. But she had not bought the sexy underthings and sleepwear in her wardrobe with the idea of enticing a man. Not any man.

If she could have chosen her sleepwear on this particular night, Tara would certainly have picked something other than the blue gown. Maybe one of those high-necked flannel atrocities that Victorian women were supposed to have worn. Not that she wanted to look horrible, but she didn't want to test her shaky resistance to Devlin. And the blue gown was not exactly calculated to cool a man's blood.

Tara immediately shook the thought away with a faint grimace. She couldn't do much about it. Either she slept in that gown or slept in the buff, and she wasn't about to do *that* with Devlin in the same bed!

Sighing faintly, she kicked off her shoes and padded barefoot across the gold carpet to the connecting bathroom. Perhaps a hot shower would help her to think more clearly. She closed the bathroom door, carefully locked it, and rapidly stripped off her clothes. She made the water as hot as she could stand it, gasping under the first steamy onslaught, and then relaxing as her body adjusted to the heat. Moments later she stepped out of the stall.

Glowing pink, she shivered in the relatively cool air and reached hastily for a towel. Only then did she realize she had left the gown in the bedroom. Muttering irritably to herself, she dried off and wrapped the towel around her, reaching for the door with one hand and maintaining a death grip on the skimpy towel with the other. She paused just outside the door, keeping her head bent as she struggled with the towel's obvious desire to obey the laws of gravity. She tried several different arrangements in an effort to keep all proper areas decently covered.

Suddenly her eyes became riveted to a pair of shiny brown shoes planted squarely about a foot from her own bare toes. Male shoes. With comical slowness her eyes slid up over neatly creased brown slacks, a cream shirt open at the throat, no tie. Of course, she thought vaguely, he had discarded the tie earlier in the evening. A strong jaw, faintly shadowed. A smiling mouth.

Smiling? Oh, damn him! It was just like him to show up at the most unreasonable time!

Her red curls—even more unruly than usual, from the steamy shower—fairly quivered with rage as her head snapped back. Glittering blue eyes met darkening slate-gray ones. Then his gaze traveled away from her face to inspect her nearly nude body in a leisurely appraisal that brought the blood rushing to her cheeks.

Wishing desperately for a larger towel, Tara managed to hold the material in place over the most critical points, and resorted to anger, her oldest and best defense against that probing, caressing stare. "Did you want something?" she demanded furiously.

"Well, now . . . *there's* a question," he drawled softly, raising his eyes to her face at last.

"You know what I meant!"

Though still darkened with an emotion she recognized all too easily, his eyes contained a glint of pure laughter. "Calm down, honey. I just came in to get my briefcase, and stopped to see the show."

"Show! Why, you—"

"You should demand a towel scene in every movie, honey," he told her, laughing loudly. "You'd bring down the house."

Tara considered abandoning the towel and lunging for his throat, but contented herself with glaring at him from a safe distance. "I can't stand sexist remarks like that, and you know it! I'm an actress, not a stripper!"

For some reason that comment amused him even more. He was still laughing as he stepped to one side and picked up his briefcase from the floor beside the dresser. Straightening, he regarded her from bright silver eyes and said, "You are really something special, honey. I can want you like my last hope of heaven and still find myself laughing at you."

The appreciation in his voice did nothing to soothe Tara's temper. Especially since she wasn't fooled into being flattered by his remark. She made an attempt to gather shreds of towel and dignity around her, and requested in an icy voice, "Please close the door on your way out." Unfortunately the command lost some of its effectiveness when she was forced to make a wild grab for a sliding corner of the towel.

Chuckling, Devlin started for the door. "Jim and I have a few things to go over tonight. I'll probably be late, so don't wait up for me."

"I hadn't planned to!" she snapped.

He paused in the open doorway and glanced back at her, the darkness of desire creeping back into his eyes. "Now, that," he murmured softly, "is a real pity." The door closed silently behind him.

A split second later a much-maligned yellow towel hit the door with an unsatisfying thud.

Several hours later Tara heard Devlin reenter the bedroom. The room was dim and shadowy, lit only by the bathroom light, which she had left on. She had been in bed for some time, lying on the far side with her back to the room, taking up as little space as possible.

Pretending to be asleep, she lay perfectly still and listened to Devlin moving quietly around the room. It became darker suddenly as the bathroom door closed. She heard the shower running and watched the moon through the wide window.

The scene that had taken place in the room earlier still occupied her mind, but she was no longer angry. The defiant and totally useless gesture of throwing her towel after Devlin's departing figure had brought her sense of humor to the rescue. Lord, she had felt like a fool, standing there stark naked, glaring at a crumpled yellow towel. She had no reason to be angry, after all. Other than that cute comment of his, Devlin had been a perfect gentleman. He hadn't even touched her.

Which annoyed Tara.

Suddenly aware that the shower had ceased, she tensed as the bathroom door opened and the light went out. Struggling to breathe deeply and evenly, she felt the other side of the bed give. At the same moment she remembered Devlin slept in the buff.

Oh, no! How was she supposed to sleep, with Devlin naked beside her? Especially when she remembered only too well . . .

"I know you aren't asleep, Tara," he said dryly. "You're as stiff as a board."

She remained stubbornly silent.

He sighed softly. "If your sense of modesty is offended, I'd like to point out that I'm wearing pajamas. Does that make you feel better?"

The mockery in his voice grated on Tara's nerves. With an exaggerated flounce she moved farther away from him, realizing belatedly that another inch would find her sleeping on the carpet. "I'd like to get some sleep, if you don't mind," she snapped.

There was a long silence, and then his voice came, flat and oddly bitter. "Shall we get it over with?"

The tone warned her. "Get . . . get what over with?"

A hard hand gripped her shoulder and flipped her over flat on her back. Before Tara could completely grasp the situation, she found Devlin looming over her in the darkness. One pajama-clad leg pinned both of hers firmly to the bed, and steely fingers held her shoulders.

"The attempted rape," he bit out icily. "That is what you've been waiting for, isn't it?"

"I . . . I don't know what you're talking about," she responded defiantly, pushing uselessly against his broad shoulders. He wouldn't budge, but since he wasn't wearing a pajama top, the contact of flesh on flesh did crazy things to her senses.

"Come off it, Tara! From the moment you realized we'd be sharing this bed, you've been expecting me to try to make love to you, haven't you?"

Using the only defense she had against him, Tara whipped up an anger she didn't feel. "Now who's using euphemisms? Love has nothing to do with it!" she told him angrily.

Devlin stiffened suddenly, and Tara realized too late that she had pushed him too far. In the same flat, bitter tone, he gritted out, "Well, I was taught never to contradict a lady . . . or to disappoint one."

And then his lips were on hers in a demanding, punishing kiss. There was desire in his kiss, but it was an angry, bitter desire, which frightened Tara. She kept her mouth firmly closed against him, pushing at the muscular shoulders and trying desperately to turn her face away from him.

But it was no use. Without hurting her, he managed to hold her still beneath him, and the pressure of his mouth forced her lips apart. His tongue intruded with shattering sensuality, hungrily exploring the sweetness of her mouth. Rough hands brushed aside the frail barrier of lace and satin to find the full curve of her breasts.

Desire threatened to drown Tara's rational thoughts, sweeping over her in scarlet waves of aching need. The small part of her that had not yet submerged was suddenly, desperately afraid, knowing that she was vulnerable as she had not been three years before, knowing that if he possessed her now, she would be inextricably tied to him in the most basic way possible for a woman . . . tied with unbreakable silken threads of love and need.

She gave a last desperate cry, but it wasn't strong enough to counteract her inflamed senses. The hands that had been pushing fruitlessly against his shoulders curled involuntarily, seeking to draw him even closer, her nails digging unconsciously into his skin. Her mouth came alive beneath the fierce pressure of his, returning the kiss with matching fire.

Her response did little to drain the anger from him. If anything, he seemed even more angry. Tara was dimly aware of his anger, aware of the bitterness that was as strong as it was incomprehensible.

But it was hard to concentrate on anything when his hands were moving over her body with sure knowledge and a hunger that even his bitterness could not hide.

His lips moved down her throat in a trail of fire, finally coming to rest on the pulse beating wildly at the base of her neck. Tara moved restlessly with a faint moan as she felt his hand sliding warmly over the thin satin covering her stomach. As if from a great distance she heard him speak, and even through the hazy curtain of desire she was conscious of being shocked.

"I asked you a question in the hospital, Tara, and I think you lied to me," he said harshly against her soft skin. "This time I want the truth." He lifted his head and stared down at her face. "Has there been anyone since me?"

Chapter 5

"W-what?" She stared dazedly up at him, seeing his face as a taut mask in the dim light.

"Has there been anyone since me?" he repeated harshly.

Stripped of any ability to lie, Tara could only shake her head, hating herself for the confession she was making. "No," she whispered painfully, "there's been no one."

He stared down at her for a long minute, and she could sense more than see his eyes probing her face for the truth. Then, in a suddenly gentle voice, he said, "Why not, Tara?"

She wanted to get angry at him for asking such a question, but this time the anger wouldn't come. Desire ebbed slowly from her body, leaving it cold and aching, and she wondered wearily if his revenge for her rejection three years ago was going to take this tormenting form. Unwilling to give him the weapon of her love, she said tightly, "I've been busy—you know that. I haven't had the time or the energy for any kind of a relationship."

"Was that the only reason?"

She frowned up at him, trying to identify the faint emotion in his voice. What was it—anxiety? Impossible, she told herself. There was no reason for Devlin to care how many men she'd been with in the past three years. Unless it was his pride. Did he want her to admit her love as a sop to his wounded ego? Had her response to him convinced him that she cared more than she would admit?

Bitterness rose in her. "If you're looking for your pound of flesh, Devlin, you can forget it. You had nothing to do with my lack of affairs."

"Pound of flesh?" Even in the darkness she saw his lips twist with wry bitterness. "You mean because you rejected me three years ago? Lord, you really don't trust me, do you?"

"Why should I?" She pushed uselessly at his shoulders yet again, becoming angry when he caught her hands and held them firmly folded over her stomach. "I trusted you three years ago, and you betrayed that trust."

She hadn't meant to say it, but since it was the truth, she made no effort to call back the words. He had betrayed her when he had interfered in her career, and she could neither forget nor forgive him for it.

"So that's it," he breathed softly. "You've convinced yourself that I betrayed you."

"I didn't have to *convince* myself." Tara sensed that he was suddenly pleased, as though he'd found the answer to an old riddle. She understood none of it. He was the most infuriating man! Angry and bitter one minute, pleased the next. Like a chameleon, he changed, bewilderingly, moment by moment.

And then, suddenly, the bitter, angry Devlin was back.

"My God, Tara—you mean you stuck a knife in me three years ago because of a lousy *film?*"

Unnerved by his blazing silver eyes, she defended herself desperately. "It wasn't the film, it was *trust!* I trusted you. I thought you understood how important my career was to me—and then you took that part away from me!"

"Damn it, Tara, didn't you stop to wonder *why* I recommended someone else for the part?" he demanded fiercely.

She stared up at him blankly, realizing abruptly that she hadn't ever asked him, hadn't even considered that there could have been a reason unconnected with their relationship. Had there been? "I— I just assumed . . ."

"What did you assume?" He was glaring down at her. "That I was so desperate for your body that I'd deliberately take a part away from you just to keep you in my bed every night?"

A vivid flush colored her cheeks, and she was suddenly grateful for the darkness. "You wanted me to quit acting. You told me so! What else was I supposed to think?"

Abruptly, he flung himself away from her to lie on his back, his body stiff with anger. "I don't care, Tara." His voice was flat and cold. "I really don't care. If that's the only reason your tiny mind can come up with, you're welcome to it."

"But if there was a reason—"

"Forget it!" he retorted bitterly. "You should have asked me then, Tara. The reason just isn't important anymore. Not to me. Now, go to sleep. We have a long day ahead of us tomorrow."

With trembling fingers Tara pulled up the lace straps of her nightgown and turned on her side, away from him, staring out the window. Had she been wrong three years ago? The possibility tormented her.

But it really didn't matter. Whatever his feelings before, she was certain Devlin hated her now. . . .

The flight from Las Vegas to Amarillo, Texas was uneventful. Tara was weary after a sleepless night, and, judging from his drawn face, Devlin hadn't gotten much rest either. He had dropped the loving-fiancé act the moment they had parted from Jim at the airport, withdrawing into himself and projecting a cold, unapproachable front.

Tara hadn't tried to approach him. Wrapped in her own gray misery, dreading the days ahead, when she would have to act the loving fiancée to a man she knew hated her, a man she loved nonetheless, Tara was unwilling to give him any further excuse to stick verbal pins in her. She didn't blame him for his anger of the night before. Looking back, she knew that she had hurt his pride by rejecting him so vehemently, and for such an uncertain reason.

But even if that misunderstanding was cleared up, Tara knew that their relationship had well and truly ended three years before. It was only now, pitch-forked abruptly back into Devlin's life, that

Tara realized why they had broken up. In spite of what she'd said the night before, she knew she was to blame for what had happened.

His interference in her career had made her angry, but at any other time she would have demanded his reasons and would probably have understood. Her anger had been fierce, unreasonable, and prompted by panic—because he had proposed. She had not known it then, or at any time during the past three years, but she knew now that she was afraid of marriage to the point of absolute terror.

The realization had come to her in the gray hours just before dawn as she lay sleepless beside Devlin. She had asked herself over and over again why she couldn't bring herself to fight for the man she loved, why she was afraid to take a chance and try to atone for her past mistakes. She was a grown woman, accustomed to fighting for what she wanted. Why couldn't she fight for Devlin? She could swallow her pride, couldn't she? Make herself vulnerable and prove to him that she loved him . . .

But fear had swept over her like a physical shock, and she had shied violently away from the thought of commitment. In a moment of painful insight she had seen a part of herself she hadn't known existed, something small and frightened that lived in the dark corners of her mind, where it could not be touched or confronted.

What was it?

"Tara?"

She started violently and looked across to the driver's seat of the small rented car to see Devlin frowning at her, his eyes shuttered.

"You're shivering. Do you want me to turn down the air conditioning?"

She looked at the gooseflesh on her arms and knew that it had been prompted by her thoughts. "I—yes, it is a little chilly. If you don't mind . . ."

"I don't mind. You should have said something," Devlin responded curtly, reaching to flip a switch.

Tara smiled a little wryly and looked out the car window to see the last of Amarillo's city streets fading out of sight behind them. It was the first conversation she had shared with Devlin since they had gotten off the plane, and she had to wonder if this would set the tone for their moments alone during the next couple of weeks.

With a faint sigh she glanced over the seat at Ah Poo's carrier in the back, reflecting absently that the cat had finally given up his frustrated howling. He hated being in the carrier. If she had been alone, Tara would probably have let Ah Poo out so that he could ride on the seat, but she knew instinctively that Devlin would have very strong views against letting a cat loose in a moving car, so she left well enough alone.

Satisfied with the cat's silence, Tara stared through the windshield, suddenly worried about her upcoming meeting with Devlin's mother and stepfather. Particularly his mother.

What kind of woman was she? Was she a formal woman, or casual? Broad-minded or straightlaced? Was she an affectionate mother, or domineering? No, Tara reflected silently, she couldn't be a domineering mother—not with a son as strong-willed as Devlin.

Would she approve of the young woman slated to become her daughter-in-law? Smoothing down the silk skirt of her dress, Tara wondered vaguely at her own desire for approval. Even the hidden, frightened part of herself desperately wanted Devlin's mother to approve of her. But why? What was that ghost in her mind that hungered for approval and affection yet shied fearfully away from any kind of commitment?

"My mother's anxious to meet you."

Tara glanced quickly at Devlin, saw the guarded look in his eyes, and realized he was trying to ease the strain between them. Eager to see the last of the stone-faced stranger who had accompanied her from Las Vegas, she responded, "Is she? When did you tell her about . . . about us? I mean—"

"I called her while I was in New York," he said casually, ignoring her stumbling. "She and Rick were very pleased." He sent her a sideways glance and then concentrated on the highway once again. "Rick is my stepfather."

"Do they know I'm an actress?" Tara looked down at the ring on her finger with a grimace, irritated with herself for her defensiveness regarding her career.

Devlin gave her a quick look. "Of course they know. They've seen most of your work, as a matter of fact. Mother says you should have received an Oscar for that drama last year."

Tara smiled in spite of herself. "My agent told me not to do that picture," she murmured. "That's why I broke with him and joined Karen Farrel's agency. I thought I'd made a mistake when she started pushing me to try out for *Celebration!*"

"You were worried about the singing?" Devlin asked shrewdly.

Tara turned sideways in the seat so she could study him. "Sure, I was worried," she admitted. "I've seen quite a few actresses fail as singers. I certainly didn't want to be one of them. But the part of Maggie was too good to pass up, so I gritted my teeth and tried to sing."

With a satisfied smile, Devlin murmured, almost to himself, "I thought that part would appeal to you."

Tara was just about to say that apparently her singing had been good enough, when his remark suddenly penetrated. Thinking back, she wondered why Karen's insistence that she try out for the role hadn't struck her as odd before now. "You got me that part, didn't you?" she accused Devlin.

He glanced over at her, his eyes veiled again, and responded casually, "No, of course not. The casting director had the final say."

"Oh." She folded her hands in her lap. "Then there's no need to thank you."

This time the look she received was one of surprise. She had to bite back a giggle. He had been thrown by her gentle remark and suspected irony or sarcasm, but she was in no mood to explain herself. She only knew she felt suddenly light-hearted, and she had gone through far too much self-analysis during the past twenty-four hours to try to understand why.

After a moment Devlin sighed and asked, "Do you invent the rules as you go along?"

"Rules?" Tara asked innocently. "Are we playing a game?"

"One of us is."

"It isn't me." She smiled brightly, suddenly feeling much better about everything—including the troublesome gremlin inside her head.

Devlin fell silent, and Tara could almost hear the wheels turning as he attempted to understand her change of mood. In a thoughtful voice he finally muttered, "It must be lack of sleep."

Tara hesitated, then conceded. "Well, I didn't sleep much."

He grinned. "I was talking about myself. I can't think of any other reason why I'm suddenly hearing you react calmly to my interference in your career."

"Hah! Then you admit it!" she pounced.

After a startled moment he began to laugh. "I walked right into that one, didn't I?"

"You certainly did!"

Still chuckling he murmured, "All right, I admit it. I did recommend, rather strongly, that you be given the part of Maggie." He gave her an intent look. "And you aren't angry about that, are you?"

"Not a bit," she confirmed lightly.

"Mind telling me why?"

" 'Woman's at best a contradiction still,' " she quoted gaily.

"Well, that certainly answers my question."

Tara laughed softly. "What do you expect when you ask unanswerable questions?"

Devlin was smiling. "I have to guess, huh?"

She shrugged. "There's no need to make a federal case out of it. I just don't feel like getting mad today, that's all."

"You're stepping out of character, you know," Devlin told her calmly.

"I know," she responded, just as calmly. "But I'm sure it's a temporary thing, so don't get used to it." When he laughed, she glanced questioningly at him and then changed the subject abruptly, determined to keep the conversation light. "By the way, what kind of attitude should I adopt toward Julie?"

He shrugged. "I'm hoping she'll take one look at you and just pack up and go home."

"Now I see why you couldn't get out of this entanglement by yourself," Tara said with a sigh. "If you think a seventeen-year-old is going to be discouraged by the appearance of a fiancée, you can forget it. She'll just try harder, Devlin."

A corner of his mouth quivered slightly. "How will she try harder?" he asked gravely.

"Go ahead and laugh," she told him tolerantly. "You'll think it's hysterical when she pays a late-night visit to your bedroom and either cries all over you or tries to seduce you. Or both."

The horror in the glance he shot her made Tara laugh. "With her father in the house?" he asked.

"Of course, with her father in the house. With me in the picture, Devlin, she'll feel she hasn't a moment to waste." The look of consternation on his face tickled her sense of humor almost beyond bearing. Biting the inside of her lip to keep from laughing again, she added hastily, "So tell me a little about her. Does she act her age, or does she try too hard to be the kind of woman she thinks you want?"

He sighed. "Both. One moment she's a teenager in jeans and a T-shirt, the next she's wearing too much makeup and a dress that would look better on Mae West. And she has a very unnerving habit of launching herself at me with no provocation whatsoever."

"And what's your response to these unprovoked attacks?"

"I detach myself as soon as possible."

Tara laughed out loud in spite of herself, and Devlin sent her a withering glance. "I can see you're going to be a lot of help," he told her. "Well, what am I supposed to do? Turn her over my knee?"

"Don't do that," Tara advised, still laughing. "She'll be in love with you for life!"

His lips twitched again. "Maybe I should have tried that with you," he murmured whimsically.

Tara's breath caught in her throat. "We aren't talking about me," she managed to say casually, turning her head to stare out the window.

"Would it have worked, Tara?"

"If you think I'm going to tell you that, you're crazy," she answered flippantly. She felt him gazing at her profile.

"Hope springs eternal," he murmured after a moment. Before she could react, he went on calmly, "Back to Julie, then. Since you seem to understand the incomprehensible workings of a teenage girl's mind, tell me how I should discourage her."

Tara was silent for a time. She wasn't satisfied with the only plan that occurred to her, but she couldn't think of anything else. She wondered vaguely if she was going to suggest this plan because it would be the best thing for Julie— enabling her to emerge from this first serious bout with love relatively unscarred—or because Tara herself wanted the bittersweet experience of pretending that Devlin was in love with her.

"Tara?"

Hastily she looked across at him. "I suppose you'll just have to moon over me whenever she's around. And don't look at me like that. I'm not any happier about it than you are."

He turned his gaze back to the highway. "I don't suppose you can think of anything better, can you?" he asked.

Did she just imagine it, or did his voice contain a suspicious quiver? Tara's fingers tightened on the strap of the purse in her lap. She wanted to hit him with it. But that would be too dangerous while he was driving the car. So she'd just wait. One of these days she'd catch him with his back turned and just lay him out . . . and then run like hell.

"I'm afraid that's the best I can do," she replied very calmly. "But I'm open to suggestions."

"No," he murmured. "No, you're doing fine." He seemed to be having trouble controlling his expression. "But what happens if Julie pays that late-night visit you were talking about?"

"You're on your own," Tara told him flatly.

"We could nip that problem in the bud, you know." He sent her a sideways glance, a teasing glint in the silvery depths. "All we have to do—"

"I'm not sharing your bedroom, Devlin," she interrupted calmly.

"What makes you so sure I was going to suggest that?"

"Weren't you?"

"Well . . ." He smiled like a guilty boy.

Sternly Tara reminded herself that this man had

all the innocence of a shark in bloody waters. She changed the subject abruptly. "Is Julie an only child?"

Devlin considered her question, the remains of that absurdly guilty smile still playing around his mouth and a peculiar gleam shining in his eyes, which made Tara immediately wary. Then, apparently accepting her change of subject, he answered easily, "As far as I know, she is. Why?"

"Uh huh," Tara murmured, ignoring his question. "I'll bet Holman is a widower, too. Or divorced."

"When did you become psychic?" he asked with another sideways glance.

"Around you it pays to be," she answered absently, as they turned off the highway onto a two-lane road. "Are we nearly there?" Nervousness assailed her once again, and her mouth went dry.

Displaying a certain psychic ability of his own, Devlin said softly, "Don't worry. They'll love you." Without waiting for her response, he added, "Another ten minutes or so."

Tara bit her lip with faint irritation as she turned to gaze through the window. Were her feelings as transparent as they seemed to be, she wondered, or was Devlin really reading her mind? She had laughed about the possibility with Jim, but now she felt distinctly uneasy. Did Devlin know she loved him? Did he care?

Avoiding that unproductive line of thought, she concentrated on the large herd of sleek horses in the distance. They appeared to be quarter horses, mares and foals, their excellent breeding showing

in every line. "What beautiful horses," she murmured, noting whitewashed wooden fences and
lush pastures.

"They're Rick's," Devlin replied laconically.

Tara shot him a surprised look and then turned
her eyes back to the rolling meadows, which continued as far as she could see, dotted here and
there with horses. Dizzily, she wondered how many
horses Devlin's stepfather owned and whether she
was looking at a ranch the size of northern Texas.

Why hadn't he warned her? Immediately, she
realized that to Devlin an estate this size was as
ordinary as a pair of brown shoes. He had amassed
a fortune of his own during the past ten years,
while his family had been wealthy in its own right
for most of its long and colorful history.

And what was she? Just an actress, one of thou-
sands. More successful than most, perhaps, but all
she had was the name she had built for herself. She
had no idea whether her family could trace its roots
back to royalty or to horse thieves.

Her unsettled childhood had left Tara with a
sense of insecurity and inferiority that she had been
fighting most of her adult life. She had wondered
more than once if that was why she had sought a
career in film, where she could be anyone she chose
to be. Whatever the reason, her career had given
her the opportunity to meet famous and powerful
people, which she had found to be an unsettling
experience.

Her veneer of sophistication was as thin as frost,
and she knew it. Underneath that facade existed a
wary young woman who was terrified of committing a social blunder, making a tactless comment, or

bumping into the furniture. She felt uncomfortable around wealth.

It was a funny sort of reverse snobbery, but knowing that did not help Tara overcome it. She had never felt uncomfortable around Devlin, but that, she knew, was because of his natural ability to blend in with his surroundings. Still, she had always been conscious on some level of his wealth and power, had always been dimly aware of the difference in their backgrounds.

What was she doing here? How could these people accept her as a prospective in-law? She felt completely out of her depth, as tense as a drawn bow. She would never be able to cope with Devlin's act of loving devotion . . .

"Stop it, Tara."

The soft voice snapped her out of her nervous reflections, and she looked down to see one of Devlin's large hands covering her own, gripped tightly together in her lap. Blinking as she raised her eyes, she discovered that he had stopped the car just inside of what appeared to be a driveway. A large sign arched over the road, proclaiming that this was the Double L Ranch.

Devlin was sitting sideways, one arm over the steering wheel, staring at her with dark eyes. She knew that her own eyes reflected the panic churning inside her, knew that he was seeing a vulnerability in her that she had never shown before.

In that same impossibly soft voice he said, "You're getting yourself all worked up over nothing, honey. Mother and Rick will love you. I told you that."

"I don't belong here," she whispered, all her defenses down.

His hand tightened over hers. "You're beautiful, intelligent, talented, and spirited," he told her in a gentle, measured tone. "What's not to belong? You can hold your own anywhere, Tara, anywhere. You have nothing to be ashamed of. You would fit in at a diplomatic ball, a presidential dinner, a barn dance, or a royal wedding. You can hold your own with politicians, professors, soldiers, cowboys, kings, and queens. You could topple governments with a smile."

The nonsense he was saying finally got through to Tara, and she smiled at him. His hand tightened again.

"That's better. The members of my family aren't monsters, sweetheart. They won't eat you."

Tara felt a peculiar jolt as she absorbed the endearment, wondering why he had used it when there was no audience but herself. Was he trying to make her feel better? To her own surprise, one of her hands turned beneath his and clasped it briefly. "Thank you," she murmured huskily. "I'm a bit of a coward about some things."

"You hide it well." He released her hand and turned back to the wheel. "I didn't think you were the least bit insecure."

Unwilling to expose more of herself than she already had, Tara said lightly, "I'm all right now. Let's go and beard the lioness—I mean . . ." She flushed and bit her lip, but Devlin was laughing.

"I'll remind you later that you said that," he said, chuckling.

Now, what had he meant by that? Tara mused as the car continued along the side drive. Then she forgot about it. She was only just beginning to realize that Devlin had been reading her mind again, understanding her fears with uncanny insight, and she was vaguely alarmed to realize that she wasn't angry about it. And, oddly enough, she was no longer afraid of not fitting in.

Devlin stopped the car on a circular drive in front of the house, and Tara absorbed the view in silence as he got out and came around to open her door. The house was tremendous, white and stately. It had aged gracefully over the years, until now it seemed a natural part of the landscape. It was three stories high, supported by tall white columns and embellished with wide sparkling windows. Tara wondered briefly why no one had thought to drape Spanish moss from the tall trees, and her confidence lagged once again.

Devlin opened her door and extended a hand to help her out. Before she could do more than swing her legs out of the car, he said in a conspiratorial whisper, "By the way, I forgot one of your virtues when I was listing them back there."

Her hand lost in his large clasp, Tara looked up at him blankly. "What did you forget?" she whispered back.

A mischievous demon danced in his eyes. Still whispering, he told her, "You have a temper that could flay a man wearing a suit of armor."

Her confidence unaccountably restored, Tara laughed up at him and allowed him to help her the rest of the way from the car. "Temper! You call that a virtue?"

"On you even that looks good." He slammed the car door to punctuate the remark. Suddenly a shriek from the wide porch caught their attention. "Devlin!"

A tiny, well-endowed young woman wearing skintight jeans and a halter top that was a single breath away from being indecent flung herself from the third step into Devlin's arms, uttering breathy cries of excited welcome.

Julie. Her brunette hair was caught up in a tortuous mass of twists and ringlets, vaguely Greek in design and completely unsuited to both her age and her clothing. She wore heavy makeup, including thick eyeliner, which made her resemble a cross between Cleopatra and a demented panda.

Tara felt a twinge of compassion for the girl and then nearly reeled as a wave of heavy perfume wafted her way. Good lord, she thought, highly amused. Devlin must be smothering! She tried to size the girl up quickly as Devlin began trying to disentangle himself, deciding finally that Julie would probably rush away in tears before sounding the call to battle.

Tara continued to watch her fiancé's gentle attempts to remove the arms clinging around his neck and bit her lip to keep from laughing. Well, he hadn't lied to her. Mr. Devlin Bradley quite definitely had a problem. No wonder he needed help.

Freeing himself at last, Devlin took a deep breath that sounded suspiciously like a gasp for air and reached over to yank Tara closer to his side with a complete lack of gallantry. "Tara," he began, "this is Jake Holman's daughter, Julie. Julie, this is Tara Collins—my fiancée."

Tara wasn't really surprised at the blunt, graceless introduction. She had never seen Devlin so completely rattled. A glint of desperation shone in his eyes, and a lock of his disheveled dark hair fell across his forehead, giving him the appearance of a despairing poet.

Still trying to keep from laughing, Tara said unsteadily, "Hello, Julie. It's nice to meet you."

Julie looked as if she had just stepped into a nest of vipers, one of which was rearing back to bite her. She cast a betrayed, shattered glare at Devlin, burst into tears, and rushed into the house.

"I take back everything I ever said about your charming ways," Tara commented in a voice choked with laughter.

Devlin raked a hand through his hair and grimaced. "Sorry about that. They weren't supposed to arrive here until tomorrow, and I assumed Mother would break the news to her."

"Never assume anything," Tara counseled, finally gaining control over her laughter. She cocked her head to one side and studied Devlin carefully. "That's a very interesting shade of lipstick you're wearing. Not your color, though."

"Hell." He fished in the pocket of his sports jacket and produced a handkerchief. "Get it off, will you?" he asked, handing the folded square to Tara.

Tara tilted his chin to get at the bright red splotches on his neck. "She's an enthusiastic girl, isn't she?" she commented dryly.

"She's a pain in the—"

"Hold still. How am I supposed to get this off if you don't . . ."

Devlin sighed and reached up to loosen his tie. "She wears enough perfume to float a ship," he grumbled. When Tara released his chin and began to rub the several splotches on his cheek, he lifted a rueful brow. "Well, it wasn't as bad as I expected."

"The worst is yet to come." Tara turned his head slightly to dab at a spot near his ear. "For me, anyway. The next time she sees me, she'll bring all guns to bear."

"Sounds like you're expecting a war."

"At the very least. And you're the prize. Aren't you flattered?" Tara refolded his handkerchief and tucked it back in his pocket, giving him a serene smile.

Devlin stared at her for a moment, then muttered, "I should have run like a thief."

Tara ignored the comment. "There's more lipstick on your collar. It's a good thing your fiancée doesn't have a suspicious mind. That's not her color, either."

Devlin opened his mouth to respond but was interrupted by a cheerful voice from the side of the house. "Well, what a charming couple you make!"

Tara turned in surprise, seeing first her trailer parked to one side of the drive, and then a woman strolling toward them. Her first thought was a wild: That can't be Devlin's mother. But she realized immediately that the woman was indeed his mother.

She was tall and slender, and moved with the unthinking grace she must have passed along to her son. Dark auburn hair, untouched by gray and gleaming with youthful highlights, crowned her head in a braided coronet. She had the complexion of a girl, clear and unlined, with the delicate tone of a ripe peach. And gray eyes just like Devlin's glinted between long, thick lashes, as changeable and as mysterious as the sea.

Tara knew very well that Amanda Bradley Lawton was in her late fifties, but she could swear that she was looking at a woman twenty years younger.

"Mother, why didn't you warn Julie about the engagement?" Devlin demanded, removing the last doubt from Tara's mind.

"What? And miss that perfectly entertaining introduction?" Her voice was as refined and regal as the rest of her. "Don't be ridiculous, dear boy." She reached up to tug at Devlin's ear, pulling his head down so that she could kiss his cheek. After a brief hug, which her son returned enthusiastically, she released him, murmuring, "No lipstick. Tara won't have to use the handkerchief this time."

Devlin chuckled and then reached for Tara's hand, pulling her closer. "Mother, this is Tara," he said simply.

Tara found her fascinated gaze being returned by a shrewd yet friendly appraisal, and fought back an absurd impulse to curtsy.

"What a beauty you are," Amanda exclaimed with a smile, and Tara saw that Devlin had also inherited his mother's charm. Before she could respond to the compliment, she was enfolded in a warm hug as sincere and unpretentious as the woman herself. "I don't know whether to congratulate you or mourn with you for catching him, but welcome to the family anyway, Tara."

Emerging from the hug a bit breathless, and completely unstrung by the unexpected welcome, Tara stammered, "I—thank you, Mrs. Lawton."

"Amanda, my dear. Devlin, you'll have to carry

in the luggage. Josh has a cold, and I've put him to bed."

"Personally, Mother?" Devlin inquired with a wicked lift of his brows as he headed toward the trunk.

"And why not? The poor man could hardly see to stagger to his room, let alone find his pajamas. Tara, did you bring Ah Poo? I'm looking forward to meeting him."

Tara felt as if she had wandered into a movie in the middle of the second reel. Nothing made sense. Abandoning herself to fate she opened the back door and pulled out Ah Poo's carrier. "Here he is," she murmured. "Devlin said you wouldn't mind pets."

"Not when they're cats." Within a minute the temperamental feline was in Amanda's arms, purring contentedly and returning her smiling gaze with the look of slavish devotion he normally reserved for Devlin.

"Uh . . . who's Josh?" Tara ventured hesitantly.

"My butler." Amanda smiled at her. "I found him in an English pub, weeping into his ale, about ten years ago, and he's been with me ever since. A marvelous man, really, and wonderful with cats. Can you manage the cases, Devlin?"

"Yes, Mother." He slammed the trunk shut and met Tara's bewildered gaze with a smile of amusement.

"Good. I was going to sacrifice Tara. Come along, my dear." Carrying the cat, Amanda started up the steps to the house.

Barely remembering to pick up her purse and the deserted carrier, Tara followed, desperate to ask why Josh had been weeping into his ale.

Amanda led the way through the huge entrance hall. Tara was too busy listening to her fascinating hostess's gentle stream of talk to pay more than cursory attention to the polished wood floor dotted here and there with Queen Anne chairs and heavy tables on which riding whips and western hats vied for space with priceless vases and figurines of jade and ivory. Tara stepped on a Persian rug that she thought should have been hanging in a museum and thought vaguely, Persian rugs? On a ranch?

"I've put you in the west wing," Amanda was saying. "If you lose your way, just stand still and scream until someone finds you. For the first year after Rick married me, he was forever having to hunt for me. I threatened more than once to leave a trail of bread crumbs. It wouldn't have done any good, though, because Rose is a devoted house-keeper and would have cleaned them all up. Devlin was a beast to break the news to Julie like that, but it wasn't his fault that she picked him to fall in love with, so I suppose it just couldn't be helped. Poor child, she tries too hard to be grown up. Too much makeup. She looked like an owl, didn't you think?"

Untangling the remarks as best she could, Tara murmured helplessly, "I thought a panda," and heard a muffled choking sound behind them as Devlin bumped along up the stairs with the luggage.

"A panda. Yes, you're right. Devlin, dear, Rick and Jake are out in the yearling barn. That filly you wanted came up for sale last week, and Rick bought her for you, but you may need a crowbar to get her away from him now. Do you plan to have children, my dear?"

Realizing that the question was addressed to her, Tara nearly stumbled at the top of the stairs. She heard another choke behind her. "Oh, I intend to have a houseful of them," she answered defiantly.

"You don't plan to give up your career, I hope?"

"Oh, no."

"Good." Amanda sounded deeply satisfied. "I've always wanted to see Devlin cope with bottles and diapers. His father was quite good at it, as I remember—although he had an irritating habit of pushing me out of bed for the three-o'clock feeding. And I hate cold floors. I'll have a talk with Julie and see if I can calm her down. But I don't know how much good it will do. She doesn't seem to understand me very well."

"I wonder why," Devlin murmured from the rear.

"Don't mumble, dear boy. Tara looks tired. She should rest for a while." Amanda halted on the second floor and opened a door on the right. "Here we are. Why are you lagging behind, Devlin?"

"It seemed appropriate," he murmured, brushing past Tara to take her bags into the room.

"May I take him with me, my dear, and show him the rest of the house? He'll love the pool, I think."

For a moment Tara was confused as to what Amanda was referring to—Devlin or Ah Poo. Restraining herself, she said weakly, "Of course, Mrs.—uh—Amanda."

"You see, that wasn't so hard. It'll get easier with practice. Rest as long as you like, dear. We'll be serving something downstairs around four. Come along, Devlin, and don't dawdle. Rick's wild to talk to you about that filly." She strolled off down the hall.

Tara stepped inside the bedroom and gave Devlin a blank look. "Your mother . . ." she murmured dazedly.

Leaving her suitcases at the foot of the huge bed, he headed back toward the door and said in a stage whisper, "I'm not flattered by that look of astonishment on your face."

Tara bit back a giggle. "But she's marvelous!"

"I told you she wasn't a monster—or a lioness." He winked at her and then gently closed the door as he went out.

Tara stared at the heavy door for a long moment and then sank down on the bed. She gazed around the luxurious blue-and-gold room without really seeing it, flopped back on the bed, and laughed quietly until she was out of breath.

Chapter 6

Two hours later, Tara finally gave up her useless attempts to rest and scooted off the bed. She had already unpacked and put her clothes away, and had even taken the time for a quick shower in the lovely blue-tiled bath adjoining her bedroom. She'd hoped the shower would help to relax her, but that didn't turn out to be the case. If anything, it made her feel wide awake and very puzzled.

The cause of her puzzlement was Devlin. She brooded about him as she put on a pair of black slacks and a green pullover. From the moment they had gotten out of the car, she mused, Devlin had been acting . . . odd. She couldn't put her finger on exactly what the difference was. It was as if the man she had known for nearly three and a half years had suddenly assumed an unfamiliar and disturbing mask.

Or was it a mask? She sat down on the edge of the bed to put on her shoes and continued to think.

What had been the first indication that something had changed? His teasing, of course. Devlin had always been witty, but she could only remember satire and a sardonic mockery. His lighthearted, cheerful teasing had come as a surprise.

And then she must consider his helpless reaction to Julie. *That* had been a definite surprise, although Tara herself had been a bit off-balance at the time and hadn't paid much attention to it. But . . . helpless? Devlin? She had never before seen him thrown by anything or anyone.

Was it only because Julie was the daughter of an important business associate? Or did Devlin just want to convince Tara that he really did need a fiancée? Tara stared across the room with a frown. Good heavens, she was clutching at straws. Not even Devlin would be that devious, and besides, what would be the point? There was no earthly reason why he should want her here enough to play that sort of game.

His unusual behavior probably wasn't a mask at all. He was with his family now, and able to shed his all-powerful businessman image. Simple enough. Tara's knowledge of him, after all, was entirely culled from either very public or very private moments. He was bound to act a little differently around his family.

Pushing these thoughts from her mind, Tara left her room, determined to find her way downstairs without having to "stand and scream," as Amanda had advised. She located the staircase after making only one wrong turn, and was silently congratulating herself, when she realized it was the wrong staircase. What a house! she thought ruefully. Backtracking, she finally regained her bearings and discovered the stairs that she hoped would take her back to the entrance hall. They did.

Tara hesitated on the bottom step and looked around warily. Her earlier passage through this hall had left a vague impression of the general layout, but she was becoming confused by the sheer size of the house. Four sets of double doors and two separate hallways opened onto this foyer. The doors were all closed, the halls deserted, and Tara was at a loss to know where to go from here.

With a faint grimace she flipped a mental coin and started down one of the hallways. Some doors along this hall were closed and some were open. Tara glanced into the opened rooms but found no one. One of the rooms, a den, had glass doors that led out to a patio and, beyond that, a pool. The sparkle of blue water looked inviting, and Tara started forward, but a sound caught her attention.

Someone was playing a piano. Curious, she continued down the hall until she discovered a door slightly ajar. Unwilling to intrude, she pushed the door open only far enough to peek inside. The room that met her gaze might have been called the Music Room in another age, and Tara thought that the name fit. Instead of the harp, pianoforte, and other instruments that would have seemed appropriate, the room contained a vast modern stereo system, shelves of record albums, deep chairs of Spanish leather, and low tables. And a baby grand piano.

The soft, gentle sound of a popular song wafted to Tara's ears, but she didn't really hear it. She stared at Devlin's absorbed profile for a startled moment, and then her gaze dropped automatically to his long brown fingers, moving easily over the keys.

Here was yet another discovery about the man she loved, and Tara wondered how many men lived inside that skin called Devlin Bradley. She didn't know him. She didn't know him at all.

Entranced, she listened to the soft music and watched the long brown fingers as if hypnotized. Considering that he didn't have much time to practice, he was pretty good.

The last note died away into silence, and before Tara could announce her presence, Devlin began playing something else, a simple, haunting melody that sounded vaguely familiar. Tara frowned as she tried to place the elusive tune in her memory. It came to her slowly as she watched his brooding profile that there were words to the song, words she should know. And then she remembered.

Of course there were words! She had sung them not three months before, when she'd tried out for the part of Maggie in *Celebration!* No one knew who had composed the song. It was a simple, beautiful love song. Tara had been deeply moved as she'd sung it, haunted and disturbed by the aching love and bitter regret conveyed in the words and melody.

And now . . . She stared as Devlin played this unpublished piece of music as though he'd written it himself, his face filled with an unreadable expression she'd never seen before. He looked weary and sad and strangely vulnerable, like a man who had cared, did care, deeply about someone . . .

Tara's throat ached with rising emotion. Had the press been right, after all, about Devlin's interest in the blond model? What had happened between them? She remembered various remarks she'd heard during the past months about a possible marriage, and wondered what had gone wrong. Devlin had mentioned nothing about it, but . . . She studied his face and knew suddenly, instinctively, that the emotions that had compelled him to write the song still existed. He had not forgotten the woman or his love. Jealousy swept over her, but she pushed the emotion fiercely away.

It wouldn't stay away. Because she knew now why Devlin had not mentioned love when he had asked her to marry him three years ago. Even then he had loved someone else. She knew that now. That was what he had been holding back.

The last note of the song died away, leaving an aching silence. Tara swallowed hard before she could make a sound. "That was beautiful," she said huskily.

Devlin swung around on the padded bench, surprise wiping the brooding look from his face. A faint redness crept up beneath his deep tan, and his silvery eyes moved restlessly away from her intent gaze. He rose from the bench, shoving his hands into the pockets of his jeans. "I thought you'd still be resting."

Tara advanced slowly into the room, sliding her own hands into her pockets to hide their trembling. "I wasn't all that tired." She realized that she was seeing him off guard and rattled for the second

time that day, but this time she had no desire to
laugh. Instead something hurt inside her to see the
chinks in his armor and to know that they were
real. "They didn't tell me at the studio that you
wrote that song," she commented.

Something flickered in his eyes and then was
gone. He turned toward a bar set in the corner of
the room. "Drink, Tara?"

"I don't drink this early." She watched him
splash whiskey into a glass. "You never used to
either."

"Things change." He sipped the drink, still avoiding her eyes.

Tara took a deep breath. "It's no use avoiding the
subject, you know. Why don't you just admit that
you wrote the song?"

"What makes you think I wrote it?"

She waited until he looked at her, then said evenly, "The fact that it's an unpublished song. The fact
that there's no sheet music on the piano. The fact
that you played it with such . . . feeling."

Devlin looked back down at his glass, swirling
the whiskey in what almost seemed a nervous gesture. "Didn't think I had it in me, did you?" he
murmured.

"No." She smiled faintly. "It seems that there's
a great deal about you I don't know." After a
moment's hesitation she added quietly, "It's a
beautiful song, Devlin."

He shrugged. "Don't read more into it than there
is. It's just a song."

Tara's throat tightened. Was he warning her that
the song had been written for another woman? "I'm
reading nothing into it," she told him flatly.

Devlin turned to stare at her, his gaze intent and a bit puzzled. "I only meant—"

"I know what you meant." Tara heard the shrillness in her voice and made a determined effort to calm down. Summoning up all her acting ability, she went on easily, "You meant that I should mind my own business."

He continued to gaze steadily at her, as though he were trying to probe her innermost secrets, then shrugged again. "Have it your own way." Without waiting for a response, he went on casually, "Rick and Jake are getting cleaned up. Mother took off somewhere with Ah Poo. We'll all meet in the den in about an hour."

Perversely, Tara was irritated with him for changing the subject. She wandered over to the piano and tapped a couple of keys, relieved to see that her hands were now steady. "I didn't even know you played."

He remained silent for a moment, then said dryly, "We all have secrets, don't we?"

"What's that supposed to mean?" She turned to stare at him.

"Nothing sinister." His voice was mocking.

So . . . they were back to *that* Devlin. The mocking, sardonic Devlin who could cut down an opponent without raising his voice or losing his smile. Her nemesis of the past three years, the enemy she felt fairly safe with because she was too busy yelling at him to remember that she loved him.

Once again Tara retreated behind her shield of anger. "This is not going to work. You know that, don't you? We aren't going to fool anyone with the stupid charade of yours. I was seven different kinds of an idiot to let you talk me into this."

"I didn't talk you into anything, Tara." He walked calmly around the far side of the piano, and she turned to keep facing him. "All I did was offer you a deal." He set his whiskey glass down on the piano and came to stand before her. "It isn't my fault if you're too afraid to go through with it."

"Afraid! Why, you—"

"Hush!" He glanced over her shoulder at the door, which was behind her now. "Mother's coming. Make it good, now."

Before Tara could react, she found herself in Devlin's arms, being kissed ruthlessly. From a distance it probably looked like a kiss of burning passion, but for Tara it was no such thing. Devlin meant to punish her. His lips were hard, insistent. His embrace was like a steel cage.

Tara was torn between anger and bewilderment. What was she being punished for? But, despite her confused emotions, a restless ache was forming deep inside her, and she hated herself for responding to him no matter what his mood.

Her role in this masquerade forgotten, Tara pushed against his chest with both hands, desperate to escape from an embrace that was killing her by inches, destroying her ability to resist him. She tried to twist away, but he held her with his mouth and with his hands, and she was helpless under his persistent grip. The heat of passion swept through her veins, choking off the desire to escape. Slowly the hands against his chest curled into his shirt to pull him even closer.

His kiss deepened, probing and relentless, as if he intended to take everything she had to offer. As if he wanted more than she had to give. One hand slid down to her hip, drawing her even closer, and she felt the evidence of his aroused desire.

And then—quite suddenly—she was free. Devlin stepped back, his face pale, his eyes a dark and stormy gray. "You see, honey," he said very softly, "I didn't need to force you."

Tara clung to the edge of the piano and stared at him, her heart beating wildly against her ribs, trying vainly to control her ragged breathing. She glanced over her shoulder to find the doorway empty, and knew without a doubt that she'd been tricked. "Damn you!" she exclaimed, "You rotten, no-good—"

"Bastard?" he suggested, lifting a mocking brow. "Cad? Devil?"

Tara struggled, without success, to come up with a searing insult, but the best she could do was, "Opportunist!" She turned on her heel, hearing his laughter and hating him for it. But his voice stopped her at the door.

"Sure you don't want a drink, Tara?"

She half turned to give him a quelling look. Making no effort to keep her voice down, she retorted, "Only if it's in a barrel—then I can drown you in it!"

She slammed the door behind her with vicious satisfaction—and halted abruptly three steps away from Amanda, who was smiling serenely. Flushing deeply, Tara managed a weak smile. "Hi."

"You're looking better, my dear." Amanda nodded toward the closed door. "There's an old proverb about marriage, you know. Begin as you mean to go on, or something like that. I'd say you were

wise not to let Devlin have everything his own way.
He takes after his father—the pride of the devil and
the soul of a dreamer. Tame the devil, my dear,
and you'll have a marriage filled with love and
laughter. Destroy the dreamer . . . and you'll never
forgive yourself. Ah Poo's swimming in the pool,
if you want him."

Feeling a bit off balance, the way she always
felt around Amanda, Tara watched as the older
woman headed toward the staircase. She considered the other woman's words carefully, and found
a nugget of truth in them. Devlin certainly had the
pride of the devil. But the soul of a dreamer? She
shrugged the thought away and went in search of
her feline water-baby.

Not until later did she remember the haunting
song, and the woman in Devlin's past. She wondered again what had happened to part them. And,
despite the way Devlin had treated her, she wondered why some women didn't realize when they'd
struck gold . . .

While Amanda had come as a surprise to Tara,
Rick Lawton exactly fit her image of a Texas rancher.
He was tall and lanky, with sun-lightened brown
hair and a deeply tanned face. Laugh lines fanned
out from the corners of his mild eyes, and his
smile was gentle. He had a soft, drawling voice,
was obviously fond of his stepson, and adored
his wife.

Seated in the den with the rest of them, Tara
couldn't help but smile as she watched Amanda
and Rick. Their love was not dramatic, but soft and
warm and obviously very deep. They were sitting

on the sofa together, across from Tara's chair, both smiling at her.

Tara returned their smiles and forced herself to lean back, although the movement put her in closer proximity to Devlin, who was leaning against the back of her chair. She took a hasty sip of coffee and sent a guarded glance toward Jake Holman, who was standing by the fireplace. Her gaze met cold green eyes, and she wondered again at the man's hostility. Devlin must have been right when he'd told her in the hospital that Holman wanted Julie married to him.

Julie, of course, wasn't in the room.

"Have you two decided where you're going to live?" Amanda asked in her gentle voice.

Tara's coffee nearly went down the wrong way, but Devlin replied casually, "Not really. Tara usually works on the West Coast, and most of my work is there as well."

"You plan to keep working, Miss Collins?"

Holman's tone was cynical, and Tara felt Devlin stiffen behind her. Before he could say anything, she looked squarely at Holman and answered coolly, "Of course, Mr. Holman. I love my work."

"In my day a woman's work was her husband."

Tara smiled sweetly. "That day is long past, Mr. Holman, or haven't you noticed?"

Devlin chuckled, easing the tense atmosphere. "You can't fight progress, Jake. Women aren't second-class citizens anymore."

Tara was surprised that Devlin would defend her desire to work, but she was relieved when Rick said something to Holman, drawing his attention away from her. Knowing that Devlin would hear her, she murmured softly, "Sorry about that."

He leaned toward her. "Sorry about what?"

"Snapping at Holman. I know his goodwill is important to you. I'll try to be nice to him."

He was silent before saying quietly, "It's not that important, Tara."

She tilted her head back, surprised to find his face so near. "Not important? I thought that was why you were here."

"One of the reasons." He kissed her lightly. "Mother's watching."

Tara gave her bogus fiancé a sweet smile and hissed softly, "I repeat, you're an opportunist."

He smiled tenderly down at her. "Sneaky, too."

"I should be getting combat pay for this."

"Oh, is it such a hardship?" His silvery eyes gleamed down at her mockingly. "Funny, I didn't think so."

"You wouldn't." He laughed softly as she turned her gaze back to the others. Amanda was smiling across the room at her, and Tara returned the smile weakly, wondering just how long she was going to be able to cope with Devlin's loving attitude. How did she get herself into messes like this, anyway?

By the end of the evening Tara was convinced that the fates were punishing her for something. Devlin grew more loving and attentive by the moment, using every excuse to touch or kiss her. He had never been a particularly reticent man, and he voiced his emotions and expressed his affection no matter who happened to be present. If he was angry or humorous, it was obvious to everyone.

Apparently it was also obvious if he happened to be in love.

Aware of Amanda's shrewd, amused gaze throughout the evening, Tara was forced to go along with Devlin's determined lovemaking. He made certain that they were never alone together. She had no opportunity to relieve her feelings with a burst of temper.

Besides, no matter how much she tried to deny it to herself, she found bittersweet pleasure in pretending that he was in love . . . with her. She was wryly aware that she would have a sleepless night. Her body had always responded instantly to Devlin, and believing that he was still in love with another woman did nothing to change that. Their encounter in the music room had left her senses clamoring for satisfaction, and he wasn't, she thought angrily, helping things one damn bit!

It only got worse, of course. Julie finally made an appearance for dinner. Though she wasn't wearing war paint, she was obviously there to fight.

"I've seen some of your movies, Miss Collins," she told Tara in an innocent tone as they sat down at the table. "It's strange, though—you looked so much younger on film."

Tara couldn't help but smile at the blatant insult, but she responded cheerfully, "Yes, it's amazing what they can do with makeup these days." From the corner of her eye she saw Amanda hide a smile.

For a moment Julie looked nonplussed, but she recovered quickly. Wide-eyed, she said innocently, "I've heard so much about the wolves in Hollywood. Are those stories true? I read a newspaper article a while back that said an actress had to be willing to sleep around in order to get good parts. Is that true?"

"Julie!" The reprimand came from Holman and wasn't very strong. Julie ignored it.

"Well, is it true?" she insisted.

The topic was a sore spot with Tara, but she resisted an impulse to treat Julie like a spiteful rival rather than a teenager suffering the pangs of first love. "Only if the actress isn't talented," she replied easily, sipping her wine. "And really it usually isn't necessary," she went on, deliberately outrageous in an attempt to silence Julie. "With the new freedom and the women's movement and all, most of the men in the industry aren't that desperate."

Devlin choked slightly, but Tara ignored him and continued to smile across the table at Julie.

Maintaining her composure, the younger woman asked, "Then it isn't true what the papers wrote about you and that producer?"

"What producer?" Tara asked calmly.

"The one you went to England with last year," Julie supplied with a smug expression.

"Oh, that one." Tara shrugged indifferently. "I went to England, and he *was* with me. But then, so were a couple of dozen other people. We stayed in a terrific old castle and had to huddle together at night to keep warm. Women in one room and men in another, you know. The producer's wife was the warmest, though. She'd brought her hot-water bottle from home, and made her husband get up three times to build up the fire."

Everyone at the table laughed, and Julie looked frustrated. Descending from the heights of character assassination to the depths of childish insult, she interrupted the laughter to ask snidely, "Do you change your hair color for every film? You were a blonde in the movie you did a few months ago."

Sighing, Tara replied calmly, "No, I was wearing a wig. I was born a redhead, and a redhead I'll remain."

"You mean that's your natural color?" Julie asked with feigned surprise, as if Tara's hair were a hideous shade of purple.

"I'm afraid so," Tara murmured, honestly amused. "It *is* red, though, isn't it? My mother must have been frightened by a bottle of red ink while she was carrying me."

Julie apparently decided to give up. It was obvious she wasn't going to get a rise out of her rival. Concentrating on her dinner, she fell silent, sending Tara occasional sullen looks and glancing longingly at Devlin from time to time.

Tara sincerely wanted to make friends with the girl, but she had no opportunity to try after dinner. Devlin demanded most of her attention. He stayed as close to Tara as the hand on the end of her arm, and if he had to go farther away than that, he took her with him. He followed Tara's earlier advice to the letter, mooning over her with tender smiles and loving touches, and practically ignoring everyone else.

By ten o'clock that evening his attentions to his fiancée had approached idolatry. Amanda and Rick were amused, Holman was irritated, and Julie remained silent. Tara had a splitting headache.

Pleading her discomfort as an excuse, she headed for her room. If she heard one more "darling" from Devlin or had to utter one herself, she knew she'd wreak havoc on somebody. Probably him. A pleasant possibility to contemplate.

Devlin followed her from the room, expressing tender concern over her headache. Halfway up the stairs, and out of earshot of the others, she turned to confront him. Since she was one step ahead of him, she faced him eye to eye.

"I can tuck myself into bed alone, thank you," she told him.

His lips twitched. "Just taking a wild guess I'd say that you were mad at me."

"Bingo." She glared at him.

"I was just following your advice," he said innocently.

Tara started to tell him what he could do with her advice, then changed her mind. "Well, I've got another bit of advice for you. Watch out for dark hallways and alleys. And don't look behind you. Something may be gaining on you."

He grinned. "You, huh? With a knife?"

"With anything I can get my hands on," she replied from between clenched teeth. "If I manage to live through this—this farcical situation of yours, Devlin Bradley, I'll make the last three years seem like a tea party."

Devlin leaned against the banister and folded his arms across his chest, smiling wickedly. "Well, I've always enjoyed a good fight. And you've never disappointed me, honey."

Tara itched to throw something at him. "Damn you, quit calling me that!"

For a moment his features hardened. Then he was smiling again. "Just practicing."

"You don't need any practice," she told him flatly. "You were born to this role, Devlin. Everyone in that room would have to have been blind, deaf, and stupid not to believe that you worship the ground I walk on. So you're a success." She heard the bitterness in her voice and ignored it. "A rousing success. If you ever need a job, you won't have to knock on many doors in Hollywood."

Again his expression grew harsh, and again the mocking smile returned. "I convinced everyone but you, huh?"

"I know the truth, don't I?"

"Do you?"

She searched his face, puzzled, and found only mockery. "What's that supposed to mean?"

For a moment he seemed almost indecisive, as if he were trying to make up his mind about something. Finally he shrugged. "Nothing. Go to bed, Tara. We're both tired, and neither of us is making much sense. See you in the morning."

She turned silently and continued up the stairs, feeling his eyes on her until she reached the second-floor landing and rounded the corner. Once in her room she automatically undressed and put on the blue nightgown, reflecting absently that she was going to have to visit her trailer in the morning and find something a little warmer to wear. With the air conditioning it was cool in the room.

With effort she put the disturbing conversation with Devlin from her mind. She *was* tired—too tired to understand cryptic comments or unreadable expressions. Turning out her bedside lamp, she slid between the covers and resolutely closed her eyes, trying to ignore the ache of unfulfilled longing.

Three hours later she turned the lamp on and stared irritably at the travel alarm clock on the nightstand. 1:00 A.M. Terrific. She'd look like a hag in the morning, and wouldn't Julie have a field day with *that*. Swearing silently, she flung back the covers and got out of bed. Ah Poo, curled up on a chair in the corner of the room, blinked at her sleepily, and Tara smiled at him as she headed for her dresser. "Sorry, cat. I think I'll go for a swim."

She dressed rapidly in the yellow bikini and then found a huge towel in her bathroom. Sliding her feet into a pair of thongs, she left the room with the lamp still burning. The hallway was dimly lit, and she had no trouble this time finding her way downstairs. The lower floor was dark except for the hallways, but there was enough light to locate the den and the glass doors.

Submerged lights gave the pool a blue glow and left the patio in shadow. The air was hot and still, and Tara cast a wary glance up at the sky, relieved to see stars still shining clearly. There was no sign of a storm. Dropping her towel on one of the lounges at the edge of the pool, she stepped out of her thongs and went around to where shallow steps led into the water.

The water was cool and refreshing, and she swam to the center of the pool, keeping her head above the surface, not wanting to get her hair wet.

"What the hell are you doing swimming alone at this time of night?"

Tara gasped in surprise and nearly went under. She stared toward a darkened corner of the patio from which a familiar shape emerged. "Good God! You scared the life out of me!"

"That doesn't answer my question." Devlin dove in and swam toward her, his grim face visible now and his anger obvious. "You little fool."

She glared back at him. "That's the second time you've called me a little fool. For the second time, I'm not a fool. And I'm obviously not alone."

"But you would have been if I hadn't been here." He stopped an arm's length away and began to tread water. "It's dangerous to swim alone, and you know it."

Having just noticed that the only thing he was wearing was his too-attractive skin, Tara struggled to keep her face expressionless and her voice even. "And I suppose *you* have a pact with the devil to keep you safe?"

"I'm a better swimmer than you are."

"To hear you tell it, you're better at everything than I am," she muttered irritably.

"Not quite." He grinned. "I wouldn't fill out that bikini nearly as well as you do."

Tara stared at him in exasperation. "You're maddening. Do you know that? Absolutely maddening. And just what are *you* doing out here at this time of night?" A part of her wished he'd say he couldn't sleep for thinking of her.

"I couldn't sleep. I was up until after midnight talking to Holman," he replied, "and rather than soak *his* head, I decided to soak mine."

Deflated, Tara was nevertheless perversely glad that the evening hadn't been comfortable for him either.

"Well, I could have told you that the man wasn't happy with you. You should have waited a couple of days before trying to talk business."

"Did I say we were talking business?"

"I assumed you weren't talking politics."

"As a matter of fact, we were." Devlin shook his head. "That man will talk about anything to avoid a business discussion."

"He doesn't sound like a reliable partner."

"I'm beginning to agree with you." He moved a bit closer. "Couldn't you sleep either?"

Caught off guard by the change of subject, Tara felt her stomach tighten nervously at his nearness. "I wanted a swim. Is that a crime?"

"You didn't answer my question."

"My sleeping habits are none of your business."

"Oh, no?" He reached out suddenly and pushed her completely beneath the water.

Tara came up sputtering. "Damn it—look what you've done! I didn't want to get my hair wet!"

Devlin was laughing. "You look like a furious little girl! Sorry, honey—it was an irresistible impulse."

Acting on an impulse of her own, she grabbed a handful of his hair and ducked him before he could prepare himself. This time he was the one to come up sputtering—though he was still laughing.

Tara started to swim away, but he reached out and caught her. He held her firmly against him, letting her feel the strength of his muscled body as he kept them both effortlessly afloat. Tara's legs tangled with his, and sudden heat spread through her body like wildfire. She was abruptly conscious of the late hour and the fact that they were utterly alone.

The laughter disappeared from Devlin's eyes as he stared at her. Both the droplets of water on his skin and the blue glow from the submerged floodlights gave him an alien look. A stark beauty she had never noticed before held Tara's fascinated gaze as her eyes moved slowly over his face. How odd, she mused. She had never really looked at him before.

"Tara . . ."

She barely heard the unsteady timbre of his voice, the rough note of longing, and then his mouth was on hers, his arms crushing her painfully close.

Tara resisted the kiss for a timeless moment. Warning bells went off in her head. Then her restraint became instead a fierce response, and the irritating clamor died away. Her lips parted willingly beneath his, and she slid her arms around his neck, realizing vaguely that he was steering them toward the shallow end of the pool. As their feet touched bottom and his kiss deepened, all coherent thought ceased.

Devlin pulled her even closer, one hand tangling in her damp curls, the other at the small of her back. His mouth moved hungrily on hers, eagerly, as though he had held himself in check for far too long. The probing exploration of his tongue became an act of possession, pure and simple.

Tara felt her last ties to reality slip away. Her senses reeled. The familiar ache in her loins became an unbearable agony. She wasn't even aware when he removed her bikini, top and bottom. As his lips left hers to blaze a trail down her throat, she opened her eyes to see two scraps of yellow material floating toward the edge of the pool. By then Devlin's lips were on the creamy swell of her breast, and she wouldn't have protested if the entire population of Texas had been grouped around the pool with popcorn, soft drinks, and spotlights.

"You're so beautiful," he muttered hoarsely. One hand slid down over her hips, lifting her slightly, while the other cupped a breast with trembling fingers. His lips gently teased a hardening nipple. "So beautiful . . . so sweet. Tell me you want me, Tara."

She had been half listening, on fire from his touch and bemused by his words, but his last command caught her full and undivided attention. Suddenly aware of her own actions, she untangled her fingers from his hair and pushed fiercely against the hard shoulders. "Let go of me!"

To her surprise he obeyed immediately—so quickly, in fact, that she was caught off balance and nearly went under. At the last moment she regained her balance. Painfully aware that the clear lighted water failed completely to hide her nakedness, she managed a baleful glare at the seemingly amused man standing between her and her bikini. Damn him! How could he stay so firmly in control? Could he turn desire off like a switch?

"You're still fighting, honey," he told her softly. "I'm going to have to cure you of that."

She was furious with both him and herself. "I'll fight you to the gates of hell!" she snapped.

He reached out suddenly to cup her chin, and for a moment Tara felt his long fingers bite into her flesh with a fierce anger that didn't show on his face. In that same soft, intense voice, he said, "You'll have to go farther that that, honey. Because I'll walk barefoot through hell itself, fighting every step of the way, if that's what it takes."

When he released her chin, Tara nearly went under again. Carefully edging into deeper water, she stared at him warily. "What are you talking about?" she demanded.

He chuckled and turned toward the edge of the pool. "You'll figure it out someday." Snaring the floating bikini with one hand, he casually climbed the wide, shallow steps.

Tara tried to keep a resentful glare on her face as she watched him drop the bikini on a lounge chair and pick up a towel to dry himself off, but it wasn't easy. It just wasn't fair, she thought indignantly, that a man should look so good without his clothes on! It didn't seem decent somehow. She told herself that her gaze was completely objective and analytical, but that was a lie, and she knew it.

Unabashed by his nudity, Devlin was drying his tanned body thoroughly, and Tara felt a niggling pleasure in just watching him. If Michelangelo had ever seen this man, she thought dizzily, he never would have bothered with David. Almost hypnotized, she followed the towel's motions over uncompromisingly male planes and angles, watching muscles bunch and ripple smoothly beneath the taut flesh.

Abruptly aware of his silence and of her body's response to him, she began treading water so energetically that she bobbed about like a buoy on rough seas. She attempted to mask her discomfort by calling out with sweet unconcern, "Do you have a streak of the exhibitionist in you?"

"You don't have to watch," he returned pleasantly, bending to dry his legs.

Tara bit her lip and glared at him. "Throw my bikini over here, will you?" she asked, trying to keep her voice casual.

Devlin shrugged into his robe and belted it securely, then reached down for the bikini. Holding the scraps of material negligently in two fingers, he turned to smile at her, deviltry gleaming in his eyes. "Come and get it," he invited gently.

She'd been afraid of that. Getting out of the pool would mean having to walk across twelve feet of concrete, with what dignity she could muster, before reaching either the bikini or a towel. Tara wasn't a prude, but she wasn't about to parade around stark naked in front of Devlin if she could help it.

"Please, Devlin!" she pleaded, letting her teeth chatter for effect. She wasn't really cold, but her toes were beginning to look like prunes.

He leaned casually against one of the patio tables and continued to dangle the bikini. And kept smiling.

"Damn it!" she flared. "At least have the common decency to turn your back!"

"Why?"

He uttered that one word in a completely reasonable tone of voice, which took Tara aback for a moment. "Well . . . just because!" she sputtered.

"Typical female response."

"Don't stick labels on me!"

He laughed softly. "Temper, temper. You'll boil all the water away. Come out of there before you catch your death."

"I'd like to catch yours," she muttered. "On a twenty-foot screen. In Technicolor."

"Come out of there."

"No!"

The silence lengthened, and Tara tread water stoically, trying to ignore her mental picture of Devlin fishing an overlarge prune out of the pool at some future hour. Cautiously reaching to test the state of her toes, she finally wailed softly, "I'm getting waterlogged."

"Then come out of there." His voice was filled with laughter, and Tara's temper flared once again.

"What if someone should come along?" she hissed angrily.

"It's nearly two in the morning. The only living beings still awake are us and the owls."

"If you were a gentleman—"

"Well, I'm not, so there's no use telling me what I'd do if that were the case. Come out of there."

Tara sighed with resignation and began moving toward the steps. It wasn't as if he'd never seen her naked, she assured herself, and then immediately clamped a lid on the memories that thought aroused. Gathering together every iota of poise and dignity she possessed, she started up the steps, fixing her eyes on the towel she'd brought. Halfway there, two large hands reached for the towel and slowly began to unfold it.

Startled, her gaze slid up to Devlin's face and locked there, her breath catching in her throat. It was difficult to read his expression in the dim light, but the absorbed intensity of his silvery eyes was plainly apparent as they moved slowly over her naked flesh.

Something about that look—something elemental and primitive and fiercely male—sparked a response deep within Tara. For the first time in her life, she was totally conscious of her own

womanhood. Instead of the embarrassment she'd
expected, she felt a strange pleasure in the knowledge that he found her beautiful. Keeping her eyes
fixed on his face, she covered the remaining distance
between them slowly, a sensual heat flooding her
and counteracting the chill of the night air on her
wet skin.

As she reached him, Devlin swung the large
towel behind her and hesitated, his eyes sweeping
over her again. Then he slowly pulled the ends of
the towel toward him until she stepped closer, and
they were separated only by the fabric of his robe.
Bending his head, he whispered huskily, "Lady,
you are really testing my willpower."

She tilted her head back to look up at him. "It's
probably good for your soul," she murmured, feeling a small sense of astonishment both at her
teasing words and her continued lack of embarrassment.

"It's not my soul I'm worried about," he returned
with a soft laugh.

A part of Tara knew she was playing with fire
and bound to get her fingers burned, but she no
longer cared. It had been three long years since
she'd known the joy of belonging to him, and suddenly she was tired—very, very tired—of fighting
him. She'd have the rest of her life to hate herself for
the choice she was about to make, but she would
face the consequences in the morning.

She remembered a childhood story about the
Little Mermaid, and for the first time understood
why that tragic creature had traded her tail for feet,
even knowing the pain that would come later. What
would be the price, Tara wondered, for a night spent

in Devlin's arms? Her pride? Her self-respect?

"There are stars in your eyes," he whispered.

"I know." She smiled faintly, sadly, thinking of broken dreams and impossible wishes and prices to be paid. Stars in her eyes and rocks in her head . . . and what did any of it matter?

Devlin's smile died away, and storm clouds scudded across the silvery sheen of his eyes. He made a soft, rough sound deep in his throat and bent his head to kiss her with a gentleness that shattered her last defenses.

Suddenly the night was filled with magic, and Tara gave herself up totally to its spell. Her arms slipped up around Devlin's neck, and she pressed her body against his hard length, feeling his urgent desire and glorying in it. His kiss deepened into a searing passion, his arms locking her in a fierce embrace, the feeling between them exploding with the force of an unleashed fury.

He raised his head at last, breathing roughly, his storm-darkened eyes flickering restlessly over her soft features. "Tara, honey," he muttered thickly, "I need you so much . . . let me stay with you tonight. . . ."

Her eyes answered a silent yes, and with a harshly indrawn breath, he stepped back far enough to wrap the towel around her and swing her up into his arms.

Chapter 7

Tara kept her face turned into his neck where a pulse pounded beneath his jaw, as he carried her through the dimly-lit lower floor of the house. She wondered faintly if he would go to her room or to his, but it didn't really matter. Three years of pent-up need and loneliness demanded that she spend this night with him.

All at once aware of just how far he was carrying her, she murmured indistinctly, "I'm too heavy."

His arms tightened around her. "You're as light as a feather," he told her with a husky laugh, climbing the stairs with an ease that confirmed his statement.

Content, she sighed softly, her body relaxed and languid. How wonderful he smelled, how clean and tangy and arousingly male. She was trying vaguely to decide just what "male" meant, when she realized that he had stopped.

Raising her head, she discovered that they were in the second-floor hallway at the end opposite her bedroom. She saw immediately why Devlin had halted.

Julie was coming out of a bedroom directly in front of them, a puzzled expression on her face. She was wearing a black negligee that deserved an X-rating, and when she looked up and saw them, an expression of chagrin that was almost comical in the circumstances swept over her face.

"Something I can do for you, Julie?" Devlin asked with only a trace of hoarseness in his voice, and Tara understood then that the bedroom was his.

A deep blush flooded Julie's face as she stared back at them, shock filling her eyes. Tara realized immediately that the younger woman had never even considered the possibility that Devlin's bed would be rather full of his fiancée.

"I . . . I got lost," Julie mumbled. "I was going to fix myself a snack . . ."

Devlin was kind enough to ignore the outfit obviously meant for nighttime seduction. "Down the hall to the stairs," he directed in a casual voice. "At the bottom take the hallway to the right. That will lead directly to the kitchen."

"Th-thanks." Obviously crushed, Julie started in the direction he had indicated, casting another small glance at Tara's towel-clad figure, her eyes still clouded with lingering shock.

Aware that her towel covered her decently only by the most broad-minded standards, Tara watched Julie disappear around the corner and then murmured, "I warned you." When Devlin didn't respond, she raised her gaze to his.

He was staring at her, his dark eyes hesitant, and she realized that he was afraid the encounter with Julie had altered her mood . . . and her decision. "Your place or mine?" he asked lightly, but with a ragged edge to his voice.

Beyond pretense, she whispered, "Which is closer?"

He bent his head to kiss her swiftly and carried her into his bedroom, closing the door behind them with an impatient kick. The room lay in shadow, lit only by his bathroom light. The rumpled covers on the large bed were mute testimony to his inability to sleep.

Devlin set Tara gently on her feet by the bed, his fingers reaching immediately for the towel. Tara responded by untying the sash of his robe. Towel and robe hit the floor together, and, as she went into his arms, Tara thought dreamily that nothing in the whole world felt quite as right as having this man's arms around her. Had it really been only yesterday that she had realized she loved him?

Without being conscious of movement, she felt the soft bed beneath her back and made a kittenlike sound of contentment as his lips were pressed urgently to her throat. She moved her hands over his firm back, her fingers teasing the length of his spine, and with a feeling of pleasure and power heard him groan hoarsely.

"Yes . . . touch me," he muttered thickly. "I need you to touch me, Tara." His own hands moved over her body with unsteady eagerness, his lips hard and hot against her skin.

Memory guided her touch, desire fueled her own

eagerness as she explored the bold strength of him. The way the black hair on his chest caressed her breasts and the sensual abrasiveness of his hands touching her aroused an aching familiarity. She caught a glimpse of rare molten fire in his eyes and moaned softly as his mouth captured the hardened tip of her breast.

The long years and the bitter anger between them dissolved in a flood of turbulent need. That carefully hidden, restrained part of Tara's nature surfaced with a ravenous intensity. She was starving for him, desperate to know again the full measure of his possession. The wild hunger aroused by his touch had often shocked her before, but this time she abandoned herself to it totally.

She was a grown woman, and this man knew all of her body's secrets. He had possessed her body and her mind and her heart, and she was helpless but to acknowledge her own need of him. She moved beneath him restlessly, her nails digging unconsciously into his back. And then he moved suddenly, powerfully, and she gasped, her body arching against his instinctively.

For a moment he was still, as though the simple act of possession were enough. A shudder passed through his strong length. And then he began to move in a graceful rhythm as old as mankind.

Tara moved with him, holding him, glorying in the harmony of this timeless moment. Tension spiraled within her, like a tightly coiled spring, and she buried her face in his neck with a muffled cry.

Their lovemaking was not gentle. They were tossed about on the floodwaters of a desire too long denied, storms breaking over them, around them, and within them, until finally they were left, drained and spent, as if on the shore of some distant sea.

Devlin kissed her gently as he lowered his weight beside her onto the bed, drawing her into his arms and murmuring her name softly. Suddenly a ghostly panic she had always felt at such moments swept over Tara. She tried to fight it, moving closer to him as though to seek reassurance. Did every woman have this peculiar feeling of displacement, this fear and loneliness, after making love with a man? . . . It had happened three years before, and it was happening now.

Unwilling to try to explain what she didn't understand herself, she had never confided the feeling to Devlin. But he seemed to know. His hands moved soothingly over her back in a gentle rhythm. He whispered words of comfort, and she gradually relaxed.

Sleepy, she listened to the steady beat of his heart beneath her cheek. How amazing that the hard planes and angles of his body could provide such a comfortable resting place. It was her last clear thought before sleep claimed her.

She woke sometime just before dawn and opened her eyes to see Devlin looking down at her. She read the renewed desire in his storm-darkened gaze and felt her own need flare again. Without a moment's thought or hesitation, she went eagerly into his arms.

With the sharp edge of their hunger dulled, the almost desperate urgency of their lovemaking was gone. This time they savored each touch, each kiss. Tara was deeply moved by Devlin's tenderness and driven nearly wild by the butterfly-soft caresses he lavished over her body. Her fingers and lips teased him as well, drawing shudders from his body and deep groans from his throat.

Perhaps in payment for her teasing, Devlin turned the lovemaking into a game, holding her still beneath him. His lips moved tantalizingly down her throat to her breasts, teasing without taking, inviting yet making it impossible for her to give. Over and over he refused to take what she offered, driving her out of her mind with frustration.

Eventually his own need became too great, and he finally gave in to her murmured pleas, moving to initiate the final embrace. But some tiny witch inside Tara laughed softly and refused to admit him. The witch took over, taunting him with her body, yet refusing him satisfaction. It was a dangerous game, but Tara played it as if she'd been born to the role, her feminine instinct guiding her.

Devlin responded with a soft laugh and a gentle force of his own, taking control of the game once again with a masculine demand she could not resist. She felt a wonderful satisfaction in finally giving in to him. Abandoning the game abruptly, she responded to his passion fiercely, and the tension built between them until it exploded in a shower of golden sparks.

Again the fear swept over her in the aftermath of their lovemaking, and again Devlin soothed her. Cuddled up against the warmth of his body, she wondered faintly if he even knew what she was afraid of, and then exhaustion eased her into sleep.

The sun woke her hours later, and Tara muttered with sleepy irritability as she rolled over to escape its hateful glare. Her outflung arm encountered an empty bed, and for a long moment she lay perfectly still, with her eyes closed, trying to figure out why that didn't feel right. One eye opened slowly and stared blankly at the dented pillow beside her own. And then the events of the night before flooded into her memory, and she sat bolt upright.

Her startled gaze swept the unfamiliar room until she was convinced she was alone. Automatically reaching to pull up the covers that had fallen to her waist, she noticed her yellow robe at the foot of the bed and considered it for a frowning moment before realizing that Devlin must have gotten it for her.

She was in his bedroom. Alone. And God only knew what time it was. There wasn't a clock or a watch anywhere in the room. Judging from the position of the sun, it was still morning—but not by much. And where was Devlin?

Suddenly appalled by the realization that someone could come in at any moment and find her there, Tara scrambled off the bed and put on the robe. If she could only get to her own room without anyone's seeing her, she thought hopefully, then only Devlin would know that she'd made a complete fool of herself last night. It was bad enough, *his* knowing. She had no intention of announcing to the world that she was addicted to the man. . . .

Opening the bedroom door stealthily and seeing no one, she sighed in relief and hurried out of the room. And nearly collided with Amanda. For an eternal moment Tara stood paralyzed. If there was anything more embarrassing than coming out of a man's bedroom after a night of sin and running smack into his mother, Tara didn't know what it was.

Amanda smiled in her usual gentle way. "Good morning, Tara."

Tara pulled the lapels of her robe together, trying to present a dignified front. "Good morning," she responded, smiling brightly.

Amanda held out a casual hand. "I found these by the pool when I went out for a swim earlier. Yours, I think."

Accepting the bundle of yellow bikini and thongs, Tara felt her dignity cracking. "Oh . . . thank you. I went for a swim last night."

"I hope Devlin was with you, my dear. It's very dangerous to swim alone. Is he up, by the way?"

"Devlin? Oh . . . yes, he's . . . up."

"Probably trying out that filly of his, then. Julie's very subdued this morning. Do you happen to know why?"

"Haven't the faintest idea," Tara lied stoutly.

"Oh. Well, perhaps Jake talked to the girl—although I doubt it. He's spoiled her rotten since her mother died. Poor child."

Clutching her bundle guiltily, Tara smiled politely, wondering if only divine intervention would rescue her from this mess.

But she needn't have worried. Amanda didn't ask a single awkward question. She simply smiled again, told Tara that breakfast would be served downstairs for another hour, and strolled off.

Like a robot Tara walked to her room and closed the door behind her. She threw the bundle of yellow bikini and thongs across the room with a great deal of passion and very little accuracy. "Damn you, Devlin Bradley," she hissed into the silent room, "I'll never forgive you for this."

* * *

Of course it wasn't all Devlin's fault, Tara acknowledged half an hour later as she was drying off after a shower. He had given her a choice last night—not once, but twice. First by the pool and later in the hall. Either time she could have said no and trotted away to her room alone. But she'd said yes. And gone to his room instead.

For the first time since encountering him in the pool, Tara suddenly remembered the other woman in his life. She plopped down on the foot of her bed and continued toweling her hair dry, her movements slow and preoccupied. Staring at her reflection in the dresser mirror, she wondered why she hadn't thought of the woman last night. Even if she herself weren't afraid of commitment, Devlin could never be hers. Not entirely. He had given his heart long ago to another woman.

In the mirror Tara's lips curled bitterly. Oh, they made a dandy couple all right. She loved him and was afraid to commit herself. He wanted her but loved another woman. The only relationship they could ever have would be based solely on sexual attraction. And Tara knew with dreadful certainty that another affair with Devlin was unthinkable. Last night—what had happened last night—could never happen again. It was the only way she could continue without him. And even then . . . it just might kill her anyway.

Tara understood now why people did crazy things for love. Killed for it. Died for it. Funny—she'd always believed the poems, songs, and movies about lovers were greatly exaggerated. Melodramatic. But they weren't. She couldn't see any possible way of emerging from this tangle intact and unhurt.

Tossing the towel aside, she went to the dresser, opening drawers and pulling out clothing automatically. She dressed in slacks and a western-style blouse, then decided to go down to her trailer and find her jeans.

She straightened at last and stared into the mirror. During the next few weeks she would have to act better than she had ever acted on the screen. She would have to wave her temper like a flag and convince Devlin that she considered last night a mistake. She would have to ignore her own aching need and wear her independence like an impenetrable mask. She would have to play the loving fiancée in public and hide behind a veil of mockery when they were alone.

And in a few months she would simply hand the engagement ring back to him, smile politely, and walk away ... never letting him see that she was torn and hurt.

The first step, though—the first step was facing him today. And she wasn't certain she could do it. Haunted eyes gazed back at her as she picked up a brush and ran it through her hair, as she remembered his murmured endearments of the night before. He hadn't said such things three years ago. Had he spoken the caressing words only because he'd thought she wanted to hear them?

She pushed such pointless questions from her mind and resolutely pulled on the mask she would have to wear for as long as this engagement continued. And when she looked into the mirror again, she found her face smiling and her eyes shuttered. You're a better actress than you knew, she told herself bitterly, and watched the face in the mirror lift a mocking brow.

Ten minutes later she walked through the front door, toward her trailer, having elected to skip breakfast. The trailer door was locked, and, remembering that Devlin had the keys, she walked around to the back and fished behind the license plate for a magnet holding a spare set. Once inside, she took ten more minutes to find her jeans and a few other items she might need.

Her arms full, she glanced out the window to see Devlin standing on the porch, an unusually strained look on his face as he stared toward the trailer. Trying to ignore her rapid heartbeat, Tara took a deep breath, pasted a smile on her face, and headed for the house.

She lifted a mocking eyebrow as she passed Devlin. "Afraid I'd escape?" she asked lightly.

He followed her into the house and caught her arm as she reached the first step. "Tara?" Silvery eyes intently searched her politely inquiring face. "Why do I get the feeling that last night never happened?" he finally asked.

"Hold onto that feeling," she advised calmly.

He sighed and, releasing her arm, leaned against the banister. "Okay—what's wrong?"

"Nothing much. By the way, do you know who I happened to run into this morning as I was leaving your room, after having obviously spent the night there?"

"I'll bite. Who?"

"Your mother."

His eyes narrowed sharply. "So that's it. Tara, my mother is not a fool, and she's certainly not straightlaced. As a matter of fact she'd probably be vastly surprised if she discovered we *weren't* sleeping together."

"Good for her."

"Tara . . ." His features tightened. "You and I are both well over the legal age of consent and presumably know what we're doing. So why am I getting the cold and stony this morning? As I remember," he added evenly, "the lady was willing."

"The lady made a mistake," she replied, just as evenly. "She doesn't intend to repeat it."

Devlin stared at her for a long moment, his face unreadable. Finally he said very quietly, "When are you going to get it through that stubborn, infuriating little mind of yours that we belong together?"

Her heart twisted with anguish, but she managed to reply in the same tone, "On a cold day in hell. Now, if you'll excuse me, I have to put these things away." She continued up the stairs. He didn't follow or call after her, but Tara felt his eyes boring into her back.

During the next three days Tara found plenty to occupy her mind. She swam and sunbathed, talked to Amanda, met Rose, the housekeeper, and Josh, the butler—who turned out to be the prototype of all English butlers and too dignified to weep into anybody's ale, least of all his own. She also met the foreman and half the ranch hands.

A few days later Tara spent an entire afternoon trying to talk Ah Poo down from one of the barn lofts, where he had discovered another cat, of whom he was busily engaged in making an enemy. She and Amanda also spent one morning looking for the mouse Ah Poo had found outside and brought into the house—apparently to replace Churchill.

Tara weathered one midnight thunderstorm by stuffing her ears full of cotton and pulling the covers over her head. It was a childish solution, she knew, but the best she could do.

And she tried to keep up appearances, going out of her way, for the first time in their long and stormy relationship, to avoid giving Devlin any reason to quarrel with her, only to find that he didn't need a reason. He was her public enemy again, his voice harsh and his face cold and withdrawn. If Julie hadn't been so wrapped up in her misery, she would have noticed that her rival was less of a threat these days.

Tara was well aware of the reason for Devlin's anger, but she was a bit puzzled by its intensity. It seemed out of character for him to be so upset over her refusal to share a bed with him. And she was unwilling to try to patch things up between them, because she was afraid that if he began teasing her again, she'd have a hard time keeping her promise to stay away from him.

But by the middle of the second week Tara was so miserable that she was seriously considering packing up her belongings and clearing out. She knew it was a cowardly thought, but she wasn't feeling very brave. Only the knowledge that Devlin was perfectly capable of coming after her if she broke their agreement kept her from running like a thief.

Sitting beneath an umbrella by the pool, she toyed absently with the straw in her glass of iced tea and stared out across the water. She heard a step and glanced up to see Amanda coming toward her. Immediately she pulled on a cheerful mask.

"Don't do that, Tara." Amanda sat down beside her at the table and smiled pleadingly. "Don't pretend."

Tara's smile faltered, and she looked away. "I'm supposed to be an actress," she managed with a shaky laugh.

"And you're a very good one. But it's very difficult for one woman to hide something from another. Especially when one of the women is a mother." An unusual look of worry creased Amanda's lovely face. "My dear, forgive a mother's prying, but I hate to see you and Devlin so unhappy."

Tara stirred uncomfortably. "We had a—little disagreement."

"Little?" Amanda shook her head. "I haven't seen Devlin so upset in years. And it's plain how troubled you are, too. One of you has to end it, Tara."

Tara smiled ruefully. "Meaning me?"

"I'm afraid so." Amanda laughed softly. "I warned you about his pride. He'll go on, day after day, snapping at you and everyone else, being an absolute bear. You'll either have to swallow your own pride or buy a bulletproof vest."

Tara laughed in spite of herself. "I hope you realize how well you named him. Fierce valor. Although I think devil would have done just as well. He's reminded me more than once of Lucifer himself."

"Ah . . ." Amanda smiled. "But even Lucifer was considered to be very charming before his fall from grace. So which does Devlin remind you of—Lucifer before or after the fall?"

"I'm not sure," Tara admitted helplessly. "I think it's six of one and half a dozen of the other."

Amanda laughed, then became serious. Leaning forward, she said softly, "I know you love my son, Tara. I saw that in your eyes the first day he brought you here."

Tara's gaze dropped to her clasped hands. "I didn't realize it was so obvious," she murmured.

"Of course it was . . . and is. Devlin's the type of man who'll love only once in his life, and very deeply," she went on, unknowingly driving a stake through Tara's heart. "I'm very glad that he found you, my dear."

Everything inside Tara wanted to scream: But I'm not the one he loves! Swallowing hard, she murmured, "Thank you for being so kind to me. I'm more grateful than I can say."

"You're a member of the family . . . or as good as one." Amanda leaned back with a smile. "Go and talk to him, Tara. Find a neutral subject. Ask him about the ranch he bought. I'm probably spoiling his surprise, but I'm sure he'll forgive me if discussing it helps the two of you to make up."

"Ranch?" Tara asked hesitantly. "I didn't know he had one."

"Yes. It adjoins this one. He bought it several years ago but put an army of workmen in the house only a couple of weeks ago to start remodeling. The work should be at the point now where someone will have to make decisions about carpeting, paint, paper, and the like. He'll want you to choose, of course."

Tara started to say that *her* opinion would be the last one he'd ask for, but she choked back the words and rose to her feet. "Do you know where he is now?" she asked with a defeated smile.

"Probably in the training ring. He was planning to work with that filly of his."

Tara nodded and headed in that direction, holding onto her courage as if with both hands. She waved at a couple of ranch hands who rode by, her eyes searching the sprawling complex of stables, paddocks, and connecting lanes. Finally she located the training ring, which looked exactly like three others to her, where Devlin sat astride a beautiful black horse.

Leaning against the white fence, Tara watched him easily handling the spirited horse, his hands gentle and firm on the reins, his voice calm and soothing as he spoke. As he finally dismounted, the filly tossed her head playfully and nuzzled him gently, and Tara wondered ruefully if there was a single female creature on earth he couldn't charm.

"Is there anything you can't do?" she called out as he approached, then held up a pleading hand as his brows drew together in an angry frown. "I come in peace," she called in a lighter tone.

Halting on the other side of the fence, he stared at her for a moment before his lips twitched. "I haven't been that bad, surely," he murmured.

"Worse." She watched as he turned to loosen the horse's girth. "An absolute bear. And those are your mother's words."

"I seem to remember that something provoked my anger."

Tara sighed. "Couldn't we just forget about that?

Start over, so to speak?" She grimaced slightly as he gazed at her steadily. "Your mother's worried," she added. "I don't like to see her that way."

"Is that your only reason for coming out here?" he asked evenly.

Tara shoved her hands into her jeans pockets and stared at him across the top rail of the fence. "What do you want me to say, Devlin? That I'm miserable? All right, I'm miserable! I don't like it when you snap at me the way you've been doing. I don't like pretending to your mother that we're a normal couple but just too stubborn to make up after a little spat."

"But you still won't admit that we belong together?" His voice was hard.

She dropped her eyes, suddenly very tired and bewildered. "I don't want to fight with you, Devlin," she whispered. "Please don't make me fight with you."

He reached across the top rail to gently turn up her face. "I'm not going to give up, you know," he said softly. "I'm going to get you to admit that we belong together."

"But *why?*" she demanded, hearing the note of desperation in her voice. "There's no future for us. There never has been!"

"There's a future if we want one."

She jerked away from Devlin. "Not the kind of future I want." Tara stared at him, knowing that the only future they could possibly have would consist of a brief affair shadowed by the ghost of another woman.

"You know," he said slowly, "one of these days I'm going to figure out what makes you tick. You're the most baffling woman I've ever met in my life. Just what do you want, Tara? Do you even know?"

Meeting his eyes steadily, she said quietly, "I know what I don't want."

Some of the color seemed to leave his face. "Well, thanks." He turned his back on her and began unsaddling the patient filly, the set of his shoulders clear evidence of his anger.

Tara bit her lip, knowing that she'd offended him but unwilling to call back her words. She reached across the fence to pat the filly's nose. "Beautiful horse," she murmured.

"Don't think you can go riding," Devlin said instantly without turning around. "The horses are off limits for you."

Tara's first impulse was to find a horse and immediately ride off, but she quickly squashed the childish thought. "I know," she murmured. "The doctor said no riding for a while."

"My, but we're meek today, aren't we?" he commented sardonically.

She watched him swing the saddle over the fence. "Don't be nasty, Devlin," she said, tired.

He pulled the bridle off the horse and watched as the animal trotted off. Then he turned to Tara. "My mother really got to you, didn't she?" he said in a softer voice.

Tara shrugged and avoided his eyes. "Your mother's a nice person. I like her. I don't want to see her worried."

"So you'll make peace with me to keep her happy?"

Tara was too honest to agree completely. "And to keep myself happy." She summoned up a small smile. "I haven't been sleeping well lately."

An answering smile lightened his expression for the first time. "Could be that lonely bed," he suggested gravely.

"I doubt it." She kept her voice light with effort. "I've been sleeping alone most of my life."

Still smiling, he murmured, "The problem won't go away just because you ignore it, honey."

Tara's heart skipped a beat at the endearment. She'd never expected to hear him call her that again. "Problem? What problem?" she asked, hoping to avoid it.

"Us. And there is an 'us' whether you admit it or not."

Not wanting to discuss *that* subject again, she said hastily, "Tell me about your ranch."

"Ranch?" Devlin lifted a brow and grimaced. "Mother."

Tara nodded. "She suggested it as a neutral topic. And since we seem to be a bit short on those . . ."

He stared at her for a moment, then laughed suddenly. "Okay, honey. You win this round. But I haven't thrown in the towel yet."

Aware that they'd shelved the argument rather than settled it, Tara was nonetheless relieved. "Will you show me the ranch?"

Devlin climbed easily over the fence and reached for the saddle. "Let me put this away first."

Tara nodded happily and watched him stride away toward one of the barns. Sooner or later they'd have another fight, she knew—and probably about the same thing. But she'd worry about that when it happened. Right now it felt wonderful to be on good terms with Devlin again.

Five minutes later they were seated in one of the ranch jeeps heading out across the pasture. "It's quicker this way," Devlin explained casually when Tara shot him a questioning look.

She scanned the flat green pastureland and sighed softly, sounding wistful. "Why did you buy a ranch here? Most of your work is in New York and L.A."

He shrugged. "I like the country here. As for my work, I've about decided to sell out of the New York end."

Tara half turned on the bucket seat to stare at him curiously. "But why? I thought you loved your work."

Devlin smiled with an odd expression. "What I love is the challenge. But I've found something that will probably keep me on my toes for the rest of my life. If it doesn't drive me insane, that is."

"What's that?"

He hesitated, the fingers of his right hand drumming almost nervously on the wheel. Then he answered, very softly. "You, Tara."

For an eternal moment she thought he was joking. But the determined set of his jaw swiftly convinced her he was entirely serious. "What are you talking about?" she almost whispered.

"I've been doing a lot of thinking these last few days," he answered casually. "I've decided you need someone to watch over you. And I've decided I need a wife and a home—a settled home. So sometime during the next few months I mean to convince you to marry me, Tara."

"Are you out of your mind?"

Devlin chuckled softly, not looking at her. "That

almost sounds like what you said the last time I asked you to marry me."

Cold panic gripped Tara, but she tried to fight it. She wanted to marry Devlin. Even with the ghost of another woman standing between them, she wanted desperately to be his wife. But she couldn't! She was afraid . . . and she didn't know why.

Swallowing hard, she stared at the calm man by her side and said with strained calm, "I don't want to get married."

"I know. But I'll change your mind, honey. We belong together. Your body knows that even if your mind doesn't. Tell me that the night we spent together didn't mean anything to you. Tell me that all those nights more than three years ago didn't mean anything to you."

Tara twisted the "Bradley luck" around and around on her finger. "You can't base a marriage on sex."

"We're compatible in other areas as well," Devlin replied, for all the world as though he were discussing the weather. "We're both intelligent. We share the same tastes in books and music. We even agree on major political issues. We both have a sense of humor and a temper."

"We fight all the time," Tara interrupted desperately. "What kind of marriage would that be?"

"An interesting one." He sounded amused.

Tara searched desperately for excuses. "My career—I couldn't give it up."

"I didn't ask you to give up your career." His lips twisted wryly. "Not this time."

"Then you wouldn't have a settled home. Don't you see, Devlin? Being married to an actress—"

"Tara," he interrupted calmly, "you can go on finding reasons against our marriage until doomsday, but it won't do any good. I've made up my mind."

She laughed in spite of herself. "You make it sound like an act of God!"

He grinned. "I thought your meekness was too good to last."

Ignoring his comment, Tara rubbed her forehead fretfully. "I can't decide whether you're serious or joking," she murmured incredulously.

"Entirely serious, I assure you. In fact, I have the game plan all worked out." Stopping the jeep, he turned off the engine and gestured in front of them. "Step one: the bribe."

Realizing abruptly that they had reached Devlin's ranch, Tara looked beyond a maze of wooden white fences to a cluster of barns and outbuildings. Beyond them stood a house.

Even at this distance Tara could see that it was heart-stoppingly beautiful. Surrounded by several large trees, it had been built from a combination of stone and cedar shingles, with broad expanses of tinted glass for windows. It seemed almost out of place on the flat Texas landscape . . . and yet oddly right as well.

Her eyes wide, Tara stared at the house for a long moment. Finally she turned to meet Devlin's intent gaze. "But . . . that's my house," she whispered.

Chapter 8

$\mathcal{H}\varepsilon$ nodded, smiling slightly. When she continued to stare at him uncomprehendingly, he said quietly, "We were at your apartment one night, and you had to run down to your agent's house for a script. You wouldn't let me come with you, so while you were gone I glanced through a couple of your scrapbooks. Among the newspaper clippings, reviews, and photographs was a picture of a house, cut out of a magazine." He reached out to touch her cheek in a tender gesture. "It was your dream house, wasn't it?"

"How did you know?" she murmured.

Devlin shrugged. "I just knew."

Trying to get a grip on her churning emotions, Tara conjured up a flash of spirit. "I wish you'd stop these mindreading acts of yours. They're very disconcerting."

"If I could read your mind," he told her dryly,

"I wouldn't have to resort to bribery to get you to the altar. I'd just look into that stubborn mind of yours and find out why you're so determined not to marry me."

Resolutely Tara got out of the jeep. "I'm just not going to marry you. And that's final."

Devlin got out and came around the jeep to catch her hand. Leading her to the nearest fence, he said cheerfully, "You *are* going to marry me. And *that's* final." He lifted her easily onto the fence. "Sit tight."

"I'm not helpless, you know," she muttered. "I can get down by my—" She gasped as Devlin, who had vaulted over the fence, lifted her down on the other side.

His hands still on her waist, he glanced toward the house. "The place is full of workmen, and there's probably a ton of plaster dust floating around, but at least you'll get an idea of what it'll look like. And I see the decorator's car, so you can talk to him about paint and wallpaper."

He put a possessive arm around her shoulders and started leading Tara toward the house. "Paint and wallpaper?" she repeated blankly. "Devlin, I'm not going to decorate your house."

"*Our* house. And of course you will."

"Listen to me!" Tara tried to stop, but he pulled her along relentlessly. "Devlin, I'm not going to marry you! It's a beautiful house, but—Are you listening to me?"

He wasn't. Ignoring her muttering, he led her into the house, where he introduced her to the decorator and the foreman. He then asked both men to wait for them downstairs while he took Tara upstairs to see the bedrooms.

Torn between amusement and consternation, Tara listened as he recited characteristics of each bedroom like a salesman until they reached a smaller bedroom that had already been painted a bright, sunny yellow. Leaning against the doorjamb, Devlin abandoned his sales talk to remark blandly, "The nursery."

Tara gave him a startled look. "You do plan ahead, don't you?" she muttered.

"You told my mother you wanted a houseful of kids," he said innocently.

Tara sat down on the low sill of one of the windows and stared at him. "Less than an hour ago," she began in a carefully expressionless voice, "a man bearing a faint resemblance to you glared across a fence at me, as mad as hell. Do you always change moods so quickly, or just with me? I need a scorecard to keep up with you!"

Devlin smiled at her. "You're pretty good at changing moods yourself."

Proving the truth of this observation, she snapped, "I'm *not* going to marry you, I'm *not* going to help you decorate your house, and I'm *certainly* not going to help fill up this nursery!"

"You will, in fact, do all three."

His calm statement infuriated Tara. "Moses had less confidence when he parted the Red Sea," she remarked acidly.

"Moses needed help. I don't," Devlin responded gravely.

Tara bit her lip. "Damn it, why do you do that?" she demanded in a voice that trembled in spite of her efforts to control it.

"Do what?"

Gazing at his glinting smile, she choked back another giggle. "You know very well what! Every time I get angry at you, you make me want to laugh."

Chuckling, he confessed wryly, "You have the same effect on me. Don't you see, Tara—that's why we're good for each other."

"But I'm not going to marry you!"

"Yes, you are. But first you're going to come downstairs with me and tell the decorator that he's chosen the wrong color for the breakfast nook."

Curious in spite of herself, Tara let him lead her from the room. "What's wrong with the color he chose?"

Devlin glanced over his shoulder as they started down the stairs. "It's absolutely hideous."

"Then tell *him* that," Tara suggested.

"You might like it." He draped a casual arm around her waist as they reached the bottom of the stairs, and led her toward the back of the house. "But I give you fair warning. If you *do* like the color, I'm going to demand breakfast in bed for as long as the paint lasts."

"I'm not going to marry you, you know."

"Of course you are. Although why I want to hitch my fate to a redheaded spitfire is a matter I'll have to take up with my analyst."

"I'm serious!" she wailed softly.

"We'll talk about it later—on our twenty-fifth anniversary." He dropped a distinctly husbandly kiss on her forehead and ushered her into the breakfast nook.

Tara had no intention of disputing the decorator's choice of color. Until she saw it, that is. She had an instinctive eye for color, and couldn't help exclaiming, "Oh, no—that won't do at all!"

Immediately the man brought forth samples and swatches, and Tara joined him in a huddle before realizing what she was doing. Frantically appealed to, Devlin only smiled gently and said the choice was hers. Tara was sorely tempted to borrow a hammer from one of the workmen and hit him with it.

Two hours later they exchanged compliments all around, and Tara left the house with the dim realization that she'd chosen the color scheme for practically every room in the house . . . and entirely against her will, too. Remaining silent, she allowed Devlin to help her over the fence again and into the jeep. It wasn't until he'd turned the vehicle around that she remarked dryly, "One of these days you'll have to tell me what your secret is."

"Secret?" He shot her an innocent look.

"Yes, secret! I didn't have the slightest intention of choosing colors for your house—"

"Our house."

"—but I did it anyway. Just when did you develop this knack of making me do something completely against my will?"

"I don't know, but it bodes well for my plans to get you to the altar, doesn't it?" Before she could respond to that loaded question, he added casually, "While we're at it, we might as well drive into Amarillo and pick out the furniture."

"We'll do no such thing!" she gasped.

He grinned. "I won't press my luck. Anyway, it'll be another couple of weeks before the house is ready to furnish."

Tara sighed. "You're insane."

"Was that meant as an insult or just a general observation?" he asked with interest.

"It's the truth. Take it any way you like." She looked at him with a wry expression. "I'll probably hate myself for asking this, but if the house was step one of your little plan, what's step two?"

"Oh, that's easy," he responded cheerfully. "You're going to admit that you want me."

"I beg your pardon?"

"You heard me. You've never actually admitted it, you know. But you will. I don't suppose you'd care to admit it now?"

Out of sheer perversity, Tara snapped, "I want you like I want a migraine!"

Undaunted, he went on easily, "I want you, and very badly, too. However, since you've made it clear you don't want to share my bed yet, I won't press you on that point."

"You won't?" Tara examined him suspiciously.

He gave her an absurdly guilty look. "Well, not much, anyway. I do have to argue my case, after all."

"I'm not going to marry you. . . ."

A week later Tara was repeating the same statement, with increasing desperation. She'd decided that the easiest and least painful way of dealing with Devlin's determination to marry her would be to treat the whole matter lightly. Unfortunately that attitude didn't seem to have any effect on him.

Around the others he played the loving fiancé with the same talent he'd displayed that first day, showering Tara with adoring looks and tender touches. Alone with her he was cheerful, teasing, and totally deaf to her repeated refusals to marry him. He made certain they spent nearly every moment of the day together, meeting her at her bedroom door in the morning and escorting her back every evening. With excuses that his mother was watching, or the moon was full, or it was the second Thursday of the month, he held her and kissed her.

And it was killing Tara.

Each evening she escaped to her room to sit for long moments watching her hands shake. Her dreams were disturbed by scenes in which she held gray-eyed babies in her arms, and by conflicting images of weddings at which, as the minister asked if anyone could show just cause why the marriage should not take place, a ghostly woman stood up in the back of the church and extended an accusing finger. Tara woke up frightened and uneasy, because the woman had been her.

Slowly it dawned on her just what Devlin was accomplishing by not "pressing" her to share his bed. He was slowly driving her out of her mind! Not only was she tormented by thoughts of the night they'd spent together here, but his lovemaking had also broken through the wall she'd built around the memories of their earlier relationship. And her body, having tasted the pleasures of being in his arms, gave her no peace.

As long as he'd been angry at her she'd been able to fight her desire. But, chameleonlike, he had become a lover instead. He courted her the way any woman would love to be courted, with soft words and tender kisses.

When Tara finally relieved her feelings in a burst

of anger, he only laughed and egged her on, until she was laughing too. He was the only man she had ever known who actually seemed delighted by her temper.

The house party went on for a third week and then a month. Tara found herself at loose ends during the third and fourth weeks, since Devlin was spending a great deal of time helping Rick on the ranch. She was delighted when Amanda asked for her help.

Gazing at the older woman a bit apprehensively, Tara murmured, "I'd love to help, Amanda, but I've never been to a ranch party and I don't know much about kids. What's the party for?"

"It's a back-to-school party," Amanda explained, her gray eyes gleaming with laughter. "It's for the children of the ranch hands. They all work pretty hard during the summer, but they still hate going back to school. The party seems to help a bit. Their mothers drop them off in the morning, and we keep them for the entire day. It'll take a good week to get ready for them—we'll do a lot of cooking and baking—and at *least* a week to recover!"

Tara laughed. "It sounds daunting. Where are the men while all this is going on? Hiding?"

"More or less." Amanda smiled ruefully. "Rick's already decided it's time to round up the foals and call out the vet to check them over. Would you like to bet on which day he chooses?"

Tara smiled, but she soon discovered that Amanda was right. The men avoided the house while the frantic preparations were going on, showing up for meals and not much else. Tara helped with the baking and cooking which, to her surprise, she was good at and enjoyed. She also helped in the day-to-day running of the ranch house.

At first she was surprised by the amount of work Amanda did on a regular basis. Devlin's mother was a rich man's wife, but she was far from just that. She loved people, and, what with caring for the ranch hands, their families, and local people, as well as doing community work, Amanda was a very busy lady. Tara helped with everything, finding herself at a local bazaar one day and driving into town for decorations the next. She even helped answer the phone and mail.

For the first time in her life she was happy doing something other than acting, and she was grateful to Amanda for giving her the opportunity to discover this unexpected side of herself. She was very pleased to find out that she *could* do other things.

She was in the kitchen early on the morning of the party, up to her elbows in the last batch of cookies, when Amanda came in.

"Tara, you have to see this. Come with me," she said with a smile.

Puzzled, Tara followed her through the house to the entrance hall, and burst out laughing at the sight of Ah Poo dashing about decorated with gaily colored bits of ribbon and tissue paper. "Oh, no! Where did he find that stuff?"

Amanda bent down to look under one of the tables. "Here's the box you put the leftover decorations in. He must have—What's he after now? Tara, is that . . . ?"

"It looks like—Amanda, it's that mouse again! We have to catch it before the kids get here. Ah Poo! I *told* you to leave him outside, you dratted cat! Oh, catch him, Amanda, he's heading for the stairs!"

Amazingly enough, the party came off as planned. Although she'd been nervous about dealing with the children, Tara found that her acting ability was a godsend when it came to telling stories and making up games. She had never acted before a more satisfying audience than a group of three-to-eight-year-olds, who sat in wide-eyed, breathless silence as Tara acted out a favorite fairy tale, taking all the parts herself.

By the time she carried a sleepy toddler out to the mother's car late that afternoon, Tara was actually sorry the party was over.

Still the house party continued. In fact, no one showed any signs of leaving. Occasionally Devlin talked to Jake Holman about his business deal, but he seemed in no hurry to sign a contract. One evening he drove Tara into Amarillo for a gourmet dinner and seductive dancing and treated her like a precious piece of porcelain, only to leave her at her bedroom door with a light kiss and a cheerful smile.

Tara lay awake for hours that night, contemplating several methods of committing murder and getting away with it. She spent another sleepless hour aching for Devlin's touch, her heart yearning for his love.

It wasn't possible, though, and she knew it. Devlin was still in love with that other woman—the one Tara was afraid to ask him about. He hid it well most of the time, behaving as if he were perfectly content in Tara's company. But occasionally she would turn unexpectedly to find him staring at her as though he were seeing someone else, and his eyes would be haunted.

Her heart would catch at such moments, and she would wonder with desperate pain why he was so determined to marry her. To exorcise the ghost of a love that was—whatever he believed—very much alive? Was he so willing to settle for second best?

Fearing what his answers would be, she never asked him those questions. And she never asked herself why she was so afraid of making a commitment, why the thought of marriage made her feel lost and alone . . . and very, very frightened.

So day followed day without change, their relationship filled with undercurrents of emotion that neither acknowledged openly. And then something happened that, Tara realized later, caused yet another turning point in their relationship and sounded the first real shot in her battle to understand herself.

It was such a simple thing, really. A common, ordinary event peculiar to the hot summer months. A thunderstorm announced its presence with distant angry rumbles. . . .

Tara had been tense and restless all day, instinctively knowing that the storm was coming. She excused herself early that night, deliberately taking advantage of Devlin's brief preoccupation with a phone call to slip from the den. She went up to her room and took a long hot shower, then spent a few more minutes drying her hair and filing her nails. She let Ah Poo into the room and talked to him nervously for half an hour, until he decided to go out again. She ruined one of her newly-filed nails by chewing on it and tried three times to read the first chapter of a paperback mystery.

By then the storm was approaching rapidly, and it was after midnight. Finally giving in to her fear, Tara stripped off her robe and got into bed, her flesh covered with goose bumps beneath the silky material of her long-sleeved, floor-length nightgown. Turning off the lamp on the nightstand, she lay back and listened to the sound of rain spattering fiercely against the windowpanes.

The first loud crash of thunder caught her unawares, as it always did, and she flinched. Huddled beneath the covers, she shivered violently, hating herself for her childish fear, but unable to control it. Thunder rolled across the night sky, lightning flashed with wicked fury, and Tara trembled even more. She had never understood her fear, never conquered it. In the company of others she could hide it, but alone at night, the smothering blanket of darkness lifted only by jagged lightning, fear gripped her in its steely talons and refused to be shaken loose.

Only one person knew of her terror. He had never laughed at the weakness or scoffed at it, and she had been vaguely surprised that Devlin, who displayed no fear of anything or anyone, should have understood her irrational panic. But he had. On more than one stormy night his comforting presence had made the ordeal bearable.

Tara wanted to run to Devlin now. She wanted to lie in his arms and listen to the soothing, steady beat of his heart. She wanted him, not out of sexual desire but out of a simple, instinctive need for his physical nearness. But she couldn't go to him. Her pride would not allow it. Yet as each eternal moment passed, the need to be with him grew stronger and stronger.

Another crack of thunder interrupted her thoughts, and Tara drew the covers up around her neck with a faint moan. Oh, God—he was so near, and the temptation was so hard to resist.

"Tara."

She jerked around, her wide blue eyes peering over the blankets in search of the source of the quiet voice. For one giddy moment she wondered if the storm was calling to her. And then she saw Devlin standing by her bed, his starkly masculine outline etched for her in a brilliant flash of lightning. Wearing only pajama bottoms, his silvery eyes glittering catlike in the blue light, he looked like a primitive, pagan figure. To Tara's fear-clouded mind he seemed the devil himself, spawned out of the violent night storm.

Then another flash of lightning lit the room, and she saw that Devlin was smiling gently, reassuringly. The devil image disappeared, and he was once again the safe, comforting presence she craved.

"Would you like me to stay with you for a while?" he asked softly. When she hesitated, he promised gently, "No strings, Tara."

Immediately, silently, she reached over to toss back the covers on the side of the bed nearest to him. He slid in beside her and drew her into his arms, pulling the blankets up around them to create a cocoon of warmth and safety.

Tara snuggled up to his hard male body, silently acknowledging to herself that she would have welcomed him into her bed even if there had been strings attached to his offer.

Devlin's hands moved gently over her back, and he murmured soothingly as she shivered with each crash of thunder. "You're so strong in some ways, honey," he said lightly, "and so unsure of yourself in others. I've seen you force arrogant actors and belligerent producers to back down with only a sweet smile, and you've faced a group of hostile reporters without a blink. Yet you're terrified of thunderstorms. What are you afraid of, sweetheart?"

"I—I don't know," she murmured. "The noise . . . the lightning. It just scares me."

"Have you always been afraid of storms? All your life?"

"Yes—no." She frowned as she thought back. "I think I loved storms when I was very small."

He was silent for a moment, then said on a questioning note, "Your parents were killed when you were very small, weren't they?"

"Yes."

"How were they killed, Tara?"

Puzzled by his question, she momentarily forgot the storm. "It—it was a car crash," she answered tensely.

"Tell me about it."

She stirred uneasily. "There isn't anything to tell. They were in a car and it crashed, that's all."

His lips moved gently against her temple and he murmured quietly, "There was a storm, wasn't there?"

Tara felt her mind rushing back in time to that horrible night and closed her eyes tightly. "Yes," she whispered.

"You weren't with them?"

"No, I—I'd spent the night with a friend." Thunder crashed again, and she started violently. Suddenly the words started pouring out of her mouth, as if she had no conscious ability to stop them.

"The storm woke me up, and I was lying in bed listening to the thunder. The door opened and my friend's mother came in and—and told me what— had happened. She kept telling me it was all right to cry, but I couldn't. I couldn't cry. It was like a bad dream, a nightmare, and I told myself I'd wake up soon . . . but I never did."

Devlin's arms tightened around her. "And you've been afraid of storms ever since," he pointed out gently.

Why hadn't she realized that before? Her parents had been killed on a stormy night, and a ten-year-old child had suddenly developed a fear of storms. Such a simple answer! She lifted her head to stare at him. "I never realized . . ."

How many other fears, she wondered vaguely, did she owe to her unsettled childhood? Had it been responsible for her determination to remain independent all these years? Her fear of leaning on someone else, of trusting anyone but herself? And what of her fear of marriage? She felt somehow that if she could only discover the answer to one of those questions, she would understand it all. But the answer eluded her.

Devlin smiled at her in the dim room and ran a finger down her nose. "You've stopped trembling."

"I have, haven't I?" Tara struggled to come to terms with this new knowledge of herself. She smiled at him tremulously. "You should hang out a shingle. You'd make a pretty good psychologist."

"You see what a handy husband I'd be?"

Tara wanted to tell him about the fear *that* statement elicited, in the hope that he would find a solution just as simple, but the words wouldn't come. She could only shake her head silently.

"You're stubborn. It must be that red hair. Will our children have red hair, do you think?"

"Your mother has auburn hair, so it's likely that—" Tara broke off abruptly, appalled by what she had said, and glared at him. "Why do I let you do that to me?"

"Do what?"

"Drag me into conversations I have absolutely no interest in!" she exclaimed heatedly, if not truthfully.

"I love children. Don't you?"

"Well, yes, but . . ."

"I hope the first one's a girl." His hands were moving in a disturbing pattern over her back. "What shall we name her? Something Irish. I like Irish names."

"My name's Irish," she murmured in spite of herself.

"I know. Tara—the ancient capital of the Irish kings. How many kids shall we have?"

Tara gasped as his probing fingers discovered a sensitive spot on her lower back. She tried to think straight. "We—we aren't going to have any children."

"Of course we will. At least four. Unless you have scruples about bringing children into such a crazy world?"

"There *is* that." Thunder boomed suddenly overhead, but Tara flinched only slightly, almost completely occupied by the restless ache building up inside her body. "Um . . . four? Did you say *four?*"

"Would you rather try for an even half dozen?" he asked calmly.

Tara dropped her forehead against his shoulder with a faint moan. "Oh, God, why do you *do* this to me?"

"Was that a prayer, or a question directed at me?"

"I'm not sure." She watched her fingers trace an intricate path among the dark hairs on his chest. "You should be locked up. You know that, don't you?"

"Only if they lock you up with me."

Tara opened her mouth to reply, but the room swung crazily and she found herself flat on her back, staring up at him. She barely noticed that the storm was increasing in intensity, before his lips were on hers demandingly.

Like an addict deprived too long of a particular drug, Tara was helpless to fight the rush of passion singing through her veins. Her fingers found their way into his hair and locked there. Her lips parted immediately beneath the forceful pressure of his mouth. His arms strained her close, his heart thudding unevenly against her own.

For Tara the moment had a curious unreality, a dreamlike quality of storms without and within. She felt as though she were being carried on a tidal wave, rushing faster and faster. Her eyes tightly closed, she bit her lip as Devlin's mouth moved hotly down her throat. She moaned softly as his hand found the softness of her breast through the silky gown. He pushed aside the low neckline, his lips replacing his hand, and Tara's senses reeled.

She had no thought of refusing him, would have been incapable of refusing him. She'd been crazy to think she could give this up! But gradually she began to realize that Devlin had no intention of allowing their lovemaking to progress any further.

When her hands began to wander, he caught them firmly and folded them gently over her stomach. Butterfly-light kisses covered her closed eyelids as he drew the neck of her gown closed. Tara kept her eyes shut, his breathing coming as ragged as her own in the dim room. Then she felt the bed shift and was horrified to realize that he was leaving her.

Her eyes snapped open. "Devlin?" The question she couldn't put into words was in her voice.

"Shhh . . ." He bent over to pull the blankets up around her neck and kissed her forehead tenderly, then stood up straight.

"Are—are you leaving?" she asked huskily.

"I promised no strings, honey," he replied hoarsely. "And I mean to keep my word. I'll teach you to trust me if it's the last thing I ever do."

Tara tried to tell him that trust was the last thing on her mind just then, but the words wouldn't come. She could only watch with dazed eyes as he went to the door. He turned to look across the shadowy room at her, one hand on the knob.

"You'll come to *me*, Tara," he told her softly.

"What?" Her voice was blank.

"You'll come to me next time. You'll finally admit that you want me . . . and then you'll come to me."

He smiled broadly, deviltry gleaming in his eyes. "Step two." And he walked through the door, closing it behind him.

Seconds later, shrieking like an enraged kitten, Tara threw a pillow across the room.

For a good three days Tara told herself fiercely that she'd be *damned* if she'd give him the satisfaction of knowing he was right. One A.M. on the third night found her pacing the floor of her bedroom with a vengeance.

An hour before, Devlin had left her at her door with a chaste kiss. Now she was trying mightily to think up a way to punish him for what he was doing to her. Oddly enough her fanciful plotting always ended with him in her power for the rest of his life—and in her bed. She wanted to hate him, to despise him for using her physical desire against her, but all she felt was a need and longing so strong that it almost frightened her.

How *could* he do this to her? What power did he have over her? And why could she give him her heart and her body, yet shy fearfully away from any permanent tie?

She stood in the center of her room for a long time, staring almost blindly at the door. Part of her wanted Devlin to win his little game, wanted desperately to marry him. But a frightened little gremlin still cowered in the back of her mind with stubborn resistance. Oh, what was wrong with her?

Tara looked at her lonely bed, and her pride suddenly gave way. It didn't matter. Not her own fear, not Devlin's ghostly love. She needed him. And she had the right, didn't she? Shouldn't every woman have the right to love her man? Even if he wasn't really hers? Even if . . .

With a soft curse Tara pushed the questions aside. She looked down at her peach nightgown and grimaced, knowing it was no more suitable for prowling about the house than Julie's seductive outfit of a few weeks ago had been. But then, Tara didn't have far to prowl.

The hall was dimly lit, as always, and Tara's footsteps led her unerringly to Devlin's door. She hesitated for a tense moment, her stomach filled with butterflies, then took a deep breath and went inside the bedroom. Moonlight spilled across the large bed, and her eyes followed it to where Devlin stood looking out the window.

He was wearing a robe, and his profile had a bleak, lonely look to it. He seemed a thousand miles away, but reacted immediately when the door clicked softly behind Tara. Swinging around, he stared across the room at her, and she could have sworn that his eyes lit up.

"Tara."

Her heart seemed to jump into her throat and hang there, beating madly. His voice was deep, husky, barely above a whisper. It was odd how much could be contained in a single word, she mused vaguely. The delicate scent of a wild rose. The feel of a warm spring breeze. The muted roar of a distant ocean. Magic. And filled with promise.

She walked steadily across to him, knowing instinctively that he would wait for her to say the words. He had been honest about his desire. She would find the courage to be the same.

Reaching him, she halted and looked up to search

his guarded, intent expression. She gave him a teasing smile. "I couldn't sleep," she murmured.

An answering smile shone faintly in his eyes. "Why not?" he asked softly.

"Because I wanted you and you weren't there," she whispered. "Make love to me, Devlin. Please."

He drew in a deep, shuddering breath, and then caught her swiftly in his arms, burying his face in her neck. "Thank God," he muttered hoarsely. "I was beginning to think I would give in before you did."

In spite of her raging desire, Tara laughed softly. "Getting desperate, were you?" she mocked as he lifted his head to look down at her.

"Insane is the word," he murmured. "You've been driving me slowly out of my mind for weeks." Urgent fingers smoothed aside the lacy straps of her gown, and the silky garment dropped to the floor. Unsteadily he added, "But I've got you now."

Their lovemaking was different this time. It was shattering gentleness and burning passion, desperate need and teasing playfulness. It was as if they had only this night to belong to each other, and each wanted to make the most of it. Time and again they soared to the very edge of the precipice, only to retreat, postponing the final ecstasy. And when at last they went over the brink, Tara understood why this miraculous moment was called "the little death." She felt as if she were dying, being consumed by fire. . . .

And then her fear returned. Disturbed, she trembled as Devlin held her gently. "I'm sorry . . . I don't know what's wrong with me," she whispered.

He turned her face up, his silvery eyes searching hers intently. "You really don't know, do you?"

She shook her head, and he smiled. "There's a little girl inside you," he told her tenderly. "She doesn't show her face very often, but sometimes she comes out. When we've just made love, she realizes she's lost something of herself to me. And that frightens her."

Puzzled and disturbed by what he was saying, Tara moved restlessly against him and started to speak. But Devlin laid a gentle finger over her lips and continued in a whimsical voice. "She's afraid of giving up anything of herself, afraid of being hurt. So she shows that stubborn, defiant, frightened little face and fights the woman in you."

Tara rested her cheek against his shoulder and thought about what he had said. Then in a very small voice she murmured, "That—that makes me sound emotionally retarded."

He laughed softly. "No, just confused. All we have to do is find out why that little girl is so afraid."

"We?" she inquired uneasily.

"You're going to marry me."

"No, I—"

"And I'll keep you barefoot and pregnant, and that little girl won't have *time* to be afraid." His voice contained a hint of laughter. "She'll be too busy."

"Devlin!" Tara tried to lift her head, but he held it firmly against his shoulder. "Barefoot and pregnant!" she exclaimed.

"Of course. And we'll live happily ever after."

Tara giggled in spite of herself and gave up

her useless attempts to raise her head. *Why* did he always make her laugh just when she should have been angry or offended? "That sounds like a line from a very bad movie," she told him severely.

"I'm just a romantic at heart," he responded sadly.

"I won't marry you. And you *won't* keep me barefoot and pregnant."

"Just pregnant, then."

"Oh, for God's sake," she muttered helplessly. "Are you deaf? Or just plain out of your mind?"

"Right now I'm just plain freezing. What did you do with the covers, you shameless wench?"

Tara bit back another giggle and wondered wildly if she was going insane. "I didn't do anything with them. *You* kicked them away. I remember that distinctly."

"I did no such thing."

"You did, too."

"That's character assassination. Be a good girl and pull the covers back up." He sighed comfortably. "I may never move again."

"Some people would call that lazy," she commented.

"Not if they'd just spent a delightful hour with a wildcat. Are you going to get the covers?"

"After that remark, get them yourself!" Tara could feel herself flushing vividly.

He chuckled. "I'll have to be careful when I go in swimming, because if Mother sees the scratches on my back, she's going to wonder what I've gotten myself engaged to."

"*Devlin!*"

His chuckle became a rich, delighted laugh. "I don't believe it. You're blushing! I thought that was a lost art."

"Well, it isn't!"

"I meant it as a compliment, honey." He patted her hip and complained, "It's like the fringes of the Arctic in here. Are you going to get the covers?"

"I can't. Someone has a hammerlock on my neck."

"Well, I beg your pardon, I'm sure."

Biting her lip at his offended tone, she sat up and rummaged for the covers, then yelped as he swatted her. "Damn it! If you do that one more time—"

"You sound like a wife already," he interrupted.

"What am I going to do with you?" she wailed softly as he pulled her back down beside him and arranged the covers neatly over them.

"You're going to marry me."

"Insane people are barred from marriage. I read it somewhere."

"Don't believe everything you read." He rested his chin on top of her head. "You cuddle up to me just like a kitten."

Sleep was tugging at her mind, "I'm not going to marry you, you know," Tara murmured drowsily.

"Of course you are. . . ."

The sun was shining with irritating brightness when Tara opened her eyes, and she wondered sleepily what had awakened her. She was lying on her back, close beside Devlin, with the heavy weight of his arm across her waist and his face nuzzling her neck. She yawned and came wide awake as a soft knock sounded on the door—the sound that must have awakened her. Before she could gather her wits and poke Devlin, the door opened.

Amanda laughed softly. "Oh, don't look so horrified, my dear. I'm sorry to intrude, but there's a phone call for Devlin. Long distance and important, so the man said."

Tara was mortified. "All right," she murmured. "I'll tell him."

Amanda smiled again and withdrew, and Tara began to laugh helplessly. She reached over to shake Devlin's shoulder gently. He muttered something indistinguishable and tightened his arm across her middle.

"Devlin? *Devlin*, you have to get up!" She shook him again.

He finally woke up enough to raise himself on one elbow and stare down at her groggily. "Oh, hello," he murmured, for all the world as if she were a chance acquaintance he'd just met on the street.

Tara bit back a giggle. "I know you're not at your best in the mornings, but do try to concentrate. You have to get up."

He blinked a couple of times. "What time is it? It feels like the crack of dawn."

"I don't know what time it is, but you're probably right."

"Then why should I get up? I'm much too comfortable." He dropped his head back onto the pillow and nuzzled his face into her neck again.

Tara sighed. "You have to get up because there's a phone call for you. Long distance. And important."

"Damn it, I'm supposed to be on vacation," he muttered, then sighed heavily and rolled away from her. "It'd better be important, or I'll fire whoever dragged me away from you."

"What if he doesn't work for you?"

"Then I'll have him killed."

She giggled again and watched him fight his way out of the tangled covers, then reached to reclaim her share. "Tell me something," she requested. "Why can't you ever get out of a bed without leaving it looking like a war zone?"

"Only my wife has the right to ask me that," he replied with sleepy dignity.

"I withdraw the question."

"Stubborn to the end," he murmured, bending to pick up his robe. As he shrugged into it, realization sank in, and he stared at her. "How do you know there's a phone call for me?"

"Attaboy, champ," she murmured teasingly, reaching behind her head to plump up her pillow. "I knew you'd get there eventually."

He grinned faintly, looking absurdly endearing even with his morning stubble. "Okay, so I'm a little slow in the morning. But I'm awake now, so tell me—how did you know?"

"Amanda came in to tell me."

Devlin's eyes gleamed with unholy amusement. Sinking down on the foot of the bed, he started laughing. "You really don't have much luck maintaining your dignity around Mother, do you?"

"Not much, no. And it isn't at all funny!" But she felt her own lips twitch uncontrollably.

Still grinning, he rose to his feet and belted the robe around his lean form. "You'll have to marry me now, you know. I've been shamelessly compromised!"

"Isn't the shoe on the other foot?"

"Okay, I'll make an honest woman of you, then."

"No, thank you."

He shook his head sadly. "My mother's going to think you're a scarlet woman. You know that, don't you?"

"Go answer the phone!" she said desperately.

Chapter 9

Half an hour later Tara was fully dressed and back in her own room when Devlin stuck his head in the door to say briefly that he'd have to fly to New York immediately because of a business crisis. She barely had time to nod her understanding before he was gone.

Deep in thought, Tara went downstairs. It was only a little after 7:00 A.M., and since she usually got more than five hours of sleep, she felt a bit woozy. Her stomach was churning in a strange way, and she couldn't decide whether it was because of lack of sleep or because Devlin was leaving so abruptly.

Meeting Amanda in the dining room dressed casually in slacks and a print blouse, Tara smiled as she went to the sideboard to pour herself a cup of coffee.

"Did Devlin tell you, my dear?" Amanda asked, sipping her own coffee.

"About having to fly to New York?" Tara nodded as she carried her cup to the table and sat down across from the older woman. "But will he be able to get a reservation on such short notice?"

Devlin's mother looked faintly surprised. "His manager sent the company jet. It should have landed in Amarillo by now."

"Oh." Tara stared down at her coffee with a wry smile. She had never known anyone who owned a jet. "Are the others up?" she asked a moment later.

"Jake drove into Amarillo about an hour ago with Rick to attend a cattle auction. Rick wants to add to the herd. Julie's still in bed. You were wise not to go with Devlin, Tara."

Tara blinked. "Oh. Well, he'll be busy . . ." she murmured, not wanting to admit that he hadn't asked her to go.

Amanda glanced at her watch and shook her head. "He'd better hurry. Richard sounded almost frantic. He manages the company office in New York," she added as an afterthought.

Having only a vague idea of how the corporate empire was run, Tara could only nod blankly. "It must be serious, for Richard to send the jet after Devlin."

Amanda agreed with a rueful smile. "It has to be serious. I've met Richard, and he is *not* a man to make mountains out of molehills. If anything, he's prone to understate trouble. So if he says there's trouble, it's probably nothing short of disaster."

Tara frowned down at her coffee. Had business worries been responsible for Devlin's earlier preoccupation? She wondered. Was he worried that his business was taking a nose dive after more than ten years of success? She glanced down at the ring glittering on her finger and felt a superstitious chill creep up her spine. Was it only coincidence that Devlin should run into trouble just after announcing his intention of marrying a woman he didn't love?

"Tara?" Amanda sounded concerned. "Are you all right? You're a little pale."

Tara drew her gaze away from the glittering diamond with effort. "No, I'm fine. I—I'll just miss Devlin, that's all," she murmured, saying the first thing that came to mind.

"Will you? That's nice to hear," said a calm voice behind her.

Startled, Tara glanced over her shoulder to find Devlin, looking very much a businessman, dressed in a formal suit and tie. He was handsome, formidable, and very distant. Tara couldn't read his hooded gaze and expressionless face. He carried a briefcase in one hand and was obviously on the point of leaving.

"I should be gone three or four days," he told them. "Mother, make sure Tara doesn't kidnap one of the horses and ride off into the sunset while I'm gone."

Barely hearing Amanda's amused assent, Tara stared into Devlin's eyes and found a question there. Only dimly realizing that she was taking the first step toward commitment, she answered his question with a smile. "I'll be here," she promised quietly, and felt rewarded when some of the tension left his face.

"Good," he responded in a suddenly husky voice as he bent to kiss her lightly. "Take care of yourself, sweetheart." For her ears alone, he whispered, "Try to miss me."

Tara felt the sting of tears as she watched him kiss his mother good-bye and walk out the door. For a long moment his whispered plea echoed in her mind. Did he love her after all? At least a little bit? He was willing to give her his name and his children, but was he also offering a part of his heart?

Tara excused herself, conscious of Amanda's sympathetic, understanding eyes, and went out to sit by the pool. It was already hot and hazy, but Tara didn't notice either the sweltering heat or the humidity. She was trying to figure out just what Devlin's love might mean to her. Would it give her the courage to face the fears inside herself?

Could she trust him with her own love? Could she give him her heart without being afraid that he would throw it carelessly aside one day? Or would she end up just like her mother had, trapped in a hate-filled marriage from which she found no escape? . . .

Tara gasped and buried her face in her hands, pain and fear slicing through her. Memories washed over her like acid, eating away at the barrier she had built around that frightened inner part of herself, battering at her facade of self-confidence. She wanted to stop the hateful flood, but after sixteen years the memories pushed their way relentlessly toward the surface.

Even at the age of ten Tara had known that her parents disliked each other, that hate and resentment lay just beneath the surface of their outward lives. With a child's clearsighted wisdom, she had known, too, that her father was mostly to blame. He'd been a charming, handsome man, with eyes as blue as the sea and shoulders wide and strong to carry his adoring daughter. In another age he might have been called a rake, and mothers would have warned their daughters to beware of him.

But no one had warned Tara's mother, Kathleen. She fell head over heels in love with the charming man ten years older than herself who had drifted into the small midwestern town where she lived. She'd even dropped out of school, at sixteen years old, to marry him.

Tara was born less than a year later, in another small town. Her earliest memories were of the family's pulling up stakes in the dead of night and moving on—because her father had lost another job and owed someone money or had gotten into a fistfight. She sat drowsily between her parents in their shabby car and listened to them fight, exchanging ugly, hurting words. And then there was always another small town and another school and more new friends. Until they moved once again.

Tara never became accustomed to waking up to the sound of harsh voices and shrill accusations. Adoring her father, she blamed her mother at first. But more and more often her father's good-night kisses reeked of whiskey, and the stale scent of cheap perfume clung to him like an indictment. She knew then. And she no longer pleaded to be carried on his shoulder.

She became a silent child around her parents and temperamental with others. At school she was belligerent and fiercely independent, scorning the dolls and dresses of other little girls for her scruffy jeans and tomboyish ways.

And then her parents died in a car crash, and her ten-year-old heart was torn between the fear of being alone and a confused sense of guilt that somehow she'd been responsible for her parents' deaths.

With no relatives to claim her, she began living in a long succession of foster homes. Sullen, difficult, she never remained long in any one place. Again and again she ran away, learning to take care of herself and escaping harm only by the grace of God. The authorities always found her and placed her in yet another home. She learned to swear early and took savage delight in using shocking language. Most of all, she trusted no one.

And then, seven years after the deaths of her parents, she met a very special man. A retired professor, he had been acting as dramatic coach to a small group of community players in Tara's town. Because someone dared her to do it, Tara tried out for a part in the play *The Taming of the Shrew*, and to her astonishment, she was cast as Kate.

She found that James Ellis—or "the Professor," as the students called him—was a demanding man who expected the very best from his students. For the first time in her life Tara gave her all. She was fascinated by acting and intrigued by her own talent.

The Professor pushed and prodded her, accepting no excuses for shoddy performances or temper tantrums. He talked to her about acting and his philosophy of life. And sometime during that year she became a woman—a strong-minded, independent woman, who controlled her temper more often than not and knew exactly what she wanted out of life. She wanted to be an actress . . . a good one.

And she had. But only by burying the painful memories of her childhood, relying on independence and fierce determination to get her through the tough times. No one would ever hurt her. Not ever. She wouldn't let them. She was determined to lean on no one, depend on no one but herself.

Tara returned to an awareness of her present surroundings with a jolt, suddenly aware of the intense heat, of bright light reflected off the glassy surface of the pool. She was two people, she realized dimly—woman and child. The child in her was terrified of commitment, the child who had lain trembling in a darkened bedroom, listening to two people hurl angry accusations. The child who had faced a cold and hostile world with a chip on her shoulder and a spark of temper in her eyes—and terrible fear in her heart. The child who was afraid of learning to depend on people, only to reach out one day and find them gone.

And the woman in her? The woman, she understood at last, loved Devlin Bradley and trusted him. The woman in Tara could take daily knocks with a wry smile and laugh at herself. She was intelligent and humorous and a bit cynical. And Devlin Bradley had seen and understood both sides of her all along.

Tara stared out across the water, the wonder of this new understanding shining in her eyes. The chains of her memories seemed to be snapping away from her, one by one. She was letting go of childish promises, letting go of the stubborn, defiant little girl who had clung fearfully to her separate identity. The child began to merge at last with the woman who was strong enough to give herself to the man she loved.

It was only a first step, she knew, but a big one. She would probably catch herself at odd moments wondering if Devlin would grow tired of her. Knowing that he had loved before, and deeply, she would have to learn to accept the ghost of his lost love. But she was willing to try now. For the sake of that lonely, frightened little girl, and the sake of the woman who loved so desperately, she had to try.

"Tara?"

She blinked and looked around, to find Julie standing by the patio table. The younger woman looked every inch a teenager this morning, her hair tied back with a bright ribbon, with no makeup on her face, and a very skimpy bikini on her body that was scandalous and completely in fashion. Julie looked worried.

"Are you all right? You look a little—odd." The younger woman flushed suddenly. "I'm sorry—I should have said 'Miss Collins.' "

Tara laughed heartily. "For heaven's sake, call me Tara. You're putting me ahead a generation by being so formal. And I'm fine, Julie. Really fine."

Julie set her softly playing transistor radio on the table and smiled uncertainly. "I was going to swim, but if it'll bother you . . ."

Realizing that Julie was well on her way to getting over her crush on Devlin, Tara gave her a friendly smile. "I don't mind at all."

Julie walked over toward the edge of the pool and turned suddenly. "You—you really love him, don't you?"

"I really do," Tara answered gently.

Julie nodded briefly. "I knew, right from the first," she murmured, "but I kept thinking . . . Well, I've been a witch, haven't I?"

Tara grinned. "Julie, falling in love is never easy, and when we pick the wrong person it's sheer hell. As for being nasty—well, we all have our moments."

"You're nice." Julie returned Tara's smile. "I didn't think you would be, but you are."

"Well, thank you! You're not so bad yourself."

"Thanks." Julie hesitated before mumbling, "Daddy and I are leaving in a few days, and . . . I was wondering if you could—would . . ."

"Would what?" Tara asked curiously.

Lifting her chin, Julie finished defiantly, "I was wondering if you'd give me your autograph. So that I can show the kids at school. Otherwise they'll never believe I met you."

Startled, Tara began to laugh. "Of course I will. But I hope you and your father will stay for the wedding." She was taking a chance, because she wasn't completely certain a wedding would ever take place. She wondered vaguely if Devlin would become bored when the quarry he was chasing doubled back and grabbed him.

"Will it be soon?" Julie asked shyly.

"I'm not sure." Tara smiled. "A lot depends on Devlin's business trip, but I think the wedding will be fairly soon."

Julie nodded. "I'd love to be here for it. I'll ask Daddy if we can stay."

"Please do." Reaching absently across the table to turn up Julie's radio, Tara watched as the younger woman dove into the pool. She was shocked to realize that Devlin had already been gone nearly two hours. Her thoughts returned to her childhood. Why had she suddenly faced her childhood fears?

Tara wasn't certain, but maybe what had happened the night before had something to do with it. For the first time she had admitted she wanted Devlin, realized that she needed him in a way she still didn't fully understand. But more than anything else Devlin's uncanny understanding of her had jarred a door long closed and locked within her.

More at peace with herself than she'd been in a long time, Tara sat back and listened to the popular music, wondering if Devlin really wanted her love. So far he'd just said he wanted a home and a wife—and children.

But a man didn't have to be in love to father a child, and perhaps eventually he'd feel burdened by her love. Would he be satisfied with what he thought he wanted? Would he be content with her companionship, her humor, and the desire she could offer? Or would he wake up in the night wishing that the woman beside him were someone else?

Tara pushed the painful questions aside. She *would* marry him. If he wanted her love, she would give it gladly. And if he didn't want her love, she'd try not to burden him with it. She would have his name and his children and his companionship. They would be enough. They would *have* to be enough.

He was embedded deeply in her heart.

Content at last with her decision, Tara sat back and contemplated the future with a smile. Should she give up her career? Devlin had pointedly denied any intention of asking her . . . *this* time. But did he *want* her to give it up? He'd said he wanted to live here in Texas and raise horses. Would he be happy with a wife who was forever flying off somewhere to make a film? And did she really want to do that anyway?

The timid child inside Tara suggested urgently that she keep an iron in the fire just in case marriage didn't work out, but the woman inside Tara shoved the thought away. No. She would never again base an important decision on a fear of rejection. So . . . did she *want* to go on with her career? Did she want to be separated from the man she loved, and later from their children, because of her career? Did she really *need* that form of self-expression, that outlet for her creative energies?

Tara smothered a giggle as she realized she was rapidly talking herself out of any desire to work. Her career obviously wasn't as important to her as she'd always believed. Or perhaps Devlin was just more important. She was committed to do at least one more film. After that . . . well, she'd just wait and see.

Tara watched Julie splash around in the pool and was just about to get into her suit and join her when she suddenly froze to her chair, icy-cold shock sweeping through her body. Her eyes fixed with painful intensity on the radio, she listened in horror as the announcer reported that a jet air-craft belonging to a private corporation had crashed shortly after take-off from Amarillo, en route to New York. It was not known whether there were any survivors.

No. Tara repeated the silent plea over and over again. *No!* It couldn't be Devlin, it just couldn't be!

As the announcer said he'd report further information as it came in, Tara bit back an agonized cry of protest. She looked around, dazed, knowing she should go in and tell Amanda, do *something*, but her mind wasn't working very well. Pictures of Devlin flitted through her thoughts—Devlin smiling, angry, laughing, tender, passionate, teasing. Devlin in a business suit, astride a spirited black filly, naked beside a shadowy pool. She saw him making love to her and laughing at her and swearing at her. She saw him playing a piano superbly and brooding over the memory of a love gone wrong. She saw him whimsically talking of children and cheerfully proclaiming that she was going to marry him.

And then, horribly, her imagination conjured up an image of a broken, bleeding body, and Tara closed her eyes with a ragged moan.

"Tara!" Amanda was coming toward her, her lovely face taut with the effort to control herself, her eyes gray pools of pain.

Tara was barely conscious of Julie's climbing out of the pool with a puzzled, anxious expression. She looked up as Amanda reached the table. "I just heard."

Amanda sat down across from her and reached to grip Tara's hands strongly. "There's a chance that it wasn't his plane, Tara," she told her evenly. "*Two* private jets took off for New York this morning, only a few minutes apart. The airport officials either don't know or won't say which plane went down. Rick and Jake are on their way to the airport now—I managed to reach them at the auction—and they'll let us know as soon as possible what's happened."

"It can't be him," Tara whispered. "I—I've only just found him . . . I can't lose him now."

Julie sat down beside Tara, her concerned expression indicating that she had realized what had happened. "He'll be all right, Tara," she said hoarsely. "I just know he will!"

After a long silent moment Amanda said quietly, "Let's go into the house, my dear. You look like a ghost. I think we both need a drink." Amanda murmured more soothing words as she and Julie led Tara inside to a sofa in the den. As if by magic Josh appeared with a tray of drinks. Tara looked at him with wide, blank eyes.

"Why were you weeping into your ale, Josh?" she asked clearly.

The butler cast a startled glance at Amanda and then, apparently realizing that Tara wasn't quite herself, replied, "I'd had a bit of trouble, that's all, Miss Tara."

Tara dropped her unseeing gaze to the ring on her finger. "No," she murmured, "it was more than just a bit of trouble. People don't cry that easily. I don't. I haven't cried . . . in a very long while. Not since I was a child. Oh, I cried when the director said to cry. But that wasn't real. That wasn't me. It was someone else."

"Drink this, Tara," Amanda ordered gently, placing a glass in her hand and guiding it firmly toward her lips.

Tara drank automatically and choked as the fiery spirit tore its way down her throat. Her eyes watering, she looked up to find the others regarding her in concern and managed a faint smile. "I'm sorry. I don't usually fall apart like this," she murmured. "Josh, forgive me, please. I had no business asking you such a personal question."

"I quite understand, Miss Tara." The middle-aged man smiled suddenly. "To be perfectly truthful I don't remember why I was weeping. I'd lost my job and had one too many, I suppose."

Tara smiled as he left the room and then looked up at Amanda. "It's not knowing," she murmured, her smile fading. "That's what I can't stand. Not knowing."

"Yes," Amanda agreed, sitting down beside her and patting her hand. Julie sat down on Tara's other side, still dressed in her bikini. The three women remained silent for a time, before Amanda began to talk. She chatted about the ranch, the new foals, a comical character she'd met in Amarillo one day. She talked in her usual gentle, disjointed fashion, and Tara began to grow calm.

Julie went away for a time and returned wearing slacks and a blouse. She and Tara listened silently as Amanda continued to talk casually and easily.

All three of them jumped when the phone rang.

Betraying her anxiety for the first time, Amanda leaped to her feet and rushed to answer it. "Hello? Rick, what—" An expression of heartfelt relief spread over her face. "You're sure? Oh, thank God! Yes, I'm fine. And—and the other plane? I see. No, we'll be all right. Yes. Good-bye, darling." She turned to give Tara and Julie a shaky smile. "It wasn't Devlin's plane."

Making careful movements, Tara raised her glass to her lips and downed the rest of the whiskey, scarcely gasping. "From now on," she said calmly, "he can ride the filly to New York. It may take longer, but at least he'll be closer to the ground."

They all laughed, giddy from the sudden release of tension, and all at once Tara realized it was a beautiful day. "What about the other plane?" she asked hesitantly.

Amanda smiled. "The pilot was slightly injured, that's all. He'll be fine."

The phone rang again just then, and Amanda turned to answer it. "Devlin! Yes, we heard. Had a nasty scare there for a while. Yes. No, Rick called from the airport just a minute ago. Yes, she's here. Just a moment." She held the phone out to Tara. "He wants to talk to you, my dear."

Setting her glass down on the coffee table, Tara rose to her feet and moved to take the phone, faintly surprised that her legs were able to support her. "Devlin?"

"Mother said you'd had a scare," he said huskily. "Are you all right now?"

His voice had never sounded so utterly wonderful to her, and Tara shut her eyes as a flood of warm emotions washed over her. "Yes . . . yes, I'm fine. But it was so frightening. We didn't know which plane had gone down."

Devlin sighed. "We didn't hear anything about it until we landed here in New York. I'm sorry you were worried, honey."

Tara bit her lip. "Hurry home . . . please."

"I wish I could believe you'd say that even if my mother wasn't in the room," he murmured huskily. "I'll be home in a few days. Good-bye, darling."

"Good-bye," she whispered, and slowly replaced the receiver. She turned to Amanda and Julie and announced starkly, "Just as soon as I can drag him to the altar, I'm going to marry that man."

Then she walked carefully back to the sofa, sat down, and burst into tears, crying for the first time in years. . . .

During the next four days Amanda threw herself wholeheartedly into the task of arranging a large wedding. She ignored Tara's laughing protests, insisting that she and Devlin would be married from the ranch, with proper pomp and splendor.

Tara, who had visualized a swift flight to Vegas and a simple chapel ceremony, was both startled and amused by Amanda's plans. Her future mother-in-law began calling relatives immediately, stressing the need for secrecy, to avoid undue publicity, and naming a date barely two weeks away. Tara pointed out that the groom was woefully ignorant of these proceedings and hadn't even been consulted about a date, for heaven's sake, but Amanda brushed aside these considerations as unimportant.

Abandoning herself to fate, as she generally did around Amanda, Tara stopped protesting. She was deeply touched that Amanda wanted to give her the kind of wedding mothers generally give their daughters, and she grew closer to the older woman day by day. She even got up the courage to ask Amanda to be her matron of honor and to ask Rick to give her away. She was delighted when both accepted happily.

Even Jake Holman unbent toward her, perhaps because of his daughter's changed attitude, and started talking casually about accepting Devlin's business deal. Since Devlin had mentioned his intention of selling out in New York, Tara didn't know whether the deal was still part of his plans, but she said nothing to discourage Jake.

See? Already she was learning to be a business wife, she assured herself happily.

By the fourth day plans for the wedding were almost complete, and Tara had already had one fitting for her gown. Although she was still arguing with Amanda that she herself should pay for the dress, she was already resigned to losing. At least now she knew why she never seemed able to win an argument with Devlin—he'd inherited his talent for convincing her from his mother.

Since Devlin was due back that day, Tara found it difficult to concentrate on anything—including what kind of flowers she should carry. Excusing herself to an understanding Amanda, she went for a walk, determined to quiet the butterflies in her stomach.

She toyed with the idea of saddling a horse and going for a ride, but talked herself out of it. She wasn't obeying Devlin, she insisted silently; she just didn't really feel like riding. She climbed over a fence into a deserted paddock, heading toward a pasture in the distance where a group of mares and foals grazed quietly. Then she heard the thud of hooves and realized with a start that the paddock wasn't deserted after all.

She turned swiftly to see an unfriendly looking bay horse bearing down on her, his ears pinned to his head and every tooth gleaming. It was the stallion Devlin had warned her about—the one with a peculiar hatred of women.

Tara had enough sense not to turn and run, but she took an instinctive step backward . . . and tripped. The next few seconds were a confused blur, with the horse approaching angrily and Tara too far from the fence and flat on her back besides. And then she heard a sharp whistle and sat up hastily to see that the horse had abandoned his charge and was trotting docilely back to the stable.

Devlin waved the horse inside the stable and closed the bottom half of the Dutch door, then turned to stare across at Tara. His hands on his hips, he glared at her. "You," he shouted to her with awful patience, "need a keeper."

A giddy sense of relief at his safe return swept over Tara, and she forgot all about the horse's near-attack. Jumping to her feet, she dusted off the seat of her jeans and asked lightly, "Are you applying for the job?"

Something flickered in his eyes, and he stared at her for a long moment. "Before I make a fool of myself by leaping at your offer," he said dryly, "I'd better be sure exactly what you have in mind."

Tara walked over to stand before him. "Will you marry me?" she asked gravely.

"Well, I'll be damned," he muttered blankly.

"Probably," she agreed cheerfully.

Gripping her shoulders, he gave her a gentle shake, his silvery eyes searching her expression with an eagerness that made Tara's heart leap into her heart. "I've been proposing to you for weeks—no, damn it, *years!*—and now suddenly you're proposing to me? Have you been drinking?" he demanded suspiciously.

"Nope." She smiled up at him. "I didn't hit my head when I fell, either."

"Well, thank God!" he exclaimed unsteadily, lifting her completely off her feet and delightedly swinging her around in a circle. Setting her on her feet at last, he gazed down at her flushed face with bright eyes. "What changed your mind?" he demanded huskily.

"I nearly lost you, you know," she responded a little breathlessly. Determined to keep a light tone, she went on, "After all, who would I have to fight with if you weren't around? I decided to stake my claim before you got away."

He chuckled softly, still devouring her with his eyes. "Maybe I'll almost crash more often if it takes the fight out of you this way. Whenever you're too stubborn to give in to me, I'll just plan a near-accident—"

"Oh, no, you won't!" she interrupted fiercely. "The next time you go up in a plane, I'm going with you. Besides," she went on in a mocking tone, "it wasn't really that. I just got so tired of saying no." She yelped when he swatted her lightly, and complained. "Don't bruise the bride! What would your mother say?"

"Probably that you deserved it."

"Oh, no, she wouldn't. She's planning a huge wedding, and she'll be very disappointed if I'm black and blue with bruises when all your distinguished relations see me for the first time."

"A huge wedding? Oh, no!" he groaned.

"Now's your chance to back out," she advised calmly.

"Not a chance!" he replied with reassuring promptness. He bent his head to give her a brief, hard kiss, then grabbed her hand and began leading her toward the house. "Come hell or high water, you're going to marry me. I only hope Mother hasn't invited Aunt Mary. She's deaf as a stone."

"Is she the one who lives in Baltimore? Amanda was talking to someone in Baltimore, this morning . . ."

"Oh, no!"

Chapter 10

"*What* I want to know," Devlin demanded as they climbed out of the car in front of their ranch two weeks later, "is how my mother wound up being your matron of honor."

"I asked her," Tara replied absently, shaking her head to rid herself of the last few grains of rice. She stared at the once-gleaming Mercedes, which had been slathered with shaving cream, toothpaste, and soap, and asked, "Who decorated the car?"

"Jim." Devlin grimaced as he came to stand beside her. "Didn't you see his expression during the reception?"

"No. I was busy explaining to Aunt Mary why we weren't having a honeymoon."

He studied her carefully. "There's still time to pack up and fly off somewhere . . ."

Tara shook her head firmly. "A honeymoon isn't

a place, it's a state of mind—and I want our marriage to start in this house. It'll be a good omen."

"You think we'll need all the help we can get, huh?"

"I just believe in hedging my bets," she replied calmly. "By the way, whose car is that? I've never seen it before."

"Yours. A wedding present."

Tara stared up at him. "Mine? It—it's beautiful. But you didn't have to do that, Devlin."

"I know." He lifted her easily into his arms. "I wanted to. And now, Mrs. Bradley, shall we go see how the new furniture looks?"

Trying to fight the breathless feeling that being in his arms always gave her, she confided seriously, "I'm a little worried about that Oriental dining room."

"Well, you're the one who fell in love with those fat little vases," he teased her.

Tara frowned at him as he carried her toward the house. "They weren't all little and fat. And if you didn't like them, why didn't you say something instead of just standing there smiling like an idiot?"

"Honey, after two weeks in my lonely bed," Devlin replied, chuckling, "I wouldn't have said a word if you'd decorated the house with items from the Spanish Inquisition." He bent to let her open the door and then stepped over the threshold.

"Look," Tara said conversationally, "for the past two weeks every room between yours and mine has been stuffed with *your* relatives. I wasn't about to do any nighttime prowling. And you weren't exactly breaking down any doors to get to me, either."

"I had visions of Aunt Mary's wandering into the hallway and asking what I was doing there," he confessed wryly.

Tara giggled as he set her gently on her feet, then asked a bit breathlessly, "Um ... shouldn't you wash that stuff off the car?"

He looked injured. "On my wedding day? Besides, it's not my car." Laughing at her expression, he reached behind her to shut the door. "Don't worry, honey. Mother whispered to me just before we left that she'd send someone to pick up the car and have it washed. I only hope she tells him not to disturb us."

"She will." Tara smiled up at him. "Your mother thinks of everything. She even sent her cook over here yesterday to stock the pantry and freezer with easy-to-fix meals. In case we decide to eat, she said. Wasn't that nice of her?"

"Very nice." He bent his head to nuzzle the soft scented flesh behind her ear. "I don't suppose you're hungry?" he whispered.

"Starving," Tara said innocently.

Devlin lifted his head and sighed. "You're determined to drive me out of my mind, aren't you?" he accused ruefully.

"Could I do that?" Tara slipped from his arms with a laugh and started across the foyer. "Come and see the dining room—and this time tell me what you really think!"

For the next hour they explored the entire house, ending up in the kitchen. Like children they rummaged in the pantry and freezer, settling at last on cold chicken and salads and opening a bottle of wine. They talked casually as they ate—about how the new furniture looked, about Devlin's successful business trip, about when they should fly to L.A. to clean out their respective apartments. They talked about everything except what was on both their minds.

Surprising Tara, Devlin offered to clean up the kitchen. She warned him not to break anything, then laughed at his offended expression and left him.

In their lovely gold-and-rust bedroom Tara spent a few moments wandering around with a bemused smile. She'd done it—she'd actually married him! And, except for an uncertain moment at the very beginning of the ceremony, not a qualm had disturbed her.

It was amazing, she thought, how quickly that little girl inside her had learned to handle her fears. The possibility of losing him had done it. Life without him had seemed horrifyingly blank and empty, and that fear had been stronger than the little girl's fears of rejection.

So now she was Mrs. Devlin Bradley. And she still didn't know how her husband really felt about her. More than once during the past two weeks she had seen a watchful, brooding expression on his face, a curiously guarded wariness in his eyes when he looked at her. Though she didn't know why, it hurt to have him gaze at her that way. She was afraid the ghost of his past love was troubling him, and she didn't know what to do about it. How could she fight a ghost?

Brushing such painful thoughts away, Tara glanced out the wide windows, to see that darkness had fallen, and smiled as she went to the dresser to find the negligee that had been a present from Amanda. The day before, she and her new mother-in-law had brought over from the Lawton ranch all of Devlin's and her clothing. They would have to fly to L.A. soon to get the rest of their belongings.

Tara took a shower and put on the negligee, feeling unexpectedly nervous. She turned on a dim light on the nightstand and turned back the covers of the huge bed, then frowned as she went over to pick up her watch from the dresser. Over an hour . . . and the bridegroom remained conspicuously absent.

Another bride might well have ruined her manicure and pulled out her hair, wondering what was wrong. Not being a typical bride, Tara went looking for her husband. She found him in the den downstairs, standing before the window and staring out into the darkness.

And his eyes were haunted.

Tara came slowly into the room, aware that he was too lost in thought—or in memories—to be aware of her presence. What was she going to do? Ignore the problem and hope she could somehow teach him to love her? No, she had ignored too many problems for far too long. She had to face him.

And that meant . . .

Taking a deep breath, Tara said quietly, "It might help if you told me about her, Devlin."

Startled, he turned quickly, the brooding look vanishing as though it had never existed, to be replaced by a guarded expression. He frowned slightly. "Tell you about who?"

Tara held onto her courage and answered steadily, "The woman you can't forget. The one you think about all the time. The one you wrote that song for." Her voice broke a little as she went on painfully, "I have to know, Devlin. I have to *know*."

He took a hasty step toward her and then stopped, astonishment warring with some other unreadable emotion on his face. "*You*, Tara!" he exclaimed softly, fiercely.

For an eternal moment she thought that she had heard only what she'd wanted to hear. A thousand thoughts flitted through her mind. He . . . loved her? *She* was the woman he was haunted by? "You—you love me?" she whispered.

He gave a short laugh, as if the sound were forced from him. "God in heaven, woman—why do you think I wanted to marry you?"

"You wanted a home," she murmured dazedly.

"A home with you!"

"You—you never mentioned love."

Devlin stared at her. "Because you would have run like hell," he said hoarsely. "Even though I didn't understand that maddening mind of yours, I knew you were afraid to commit yourself." His strained features softened for a moment, giving her a glimpse of something she could hardly believe. "So I gambled . . . rushed you into marriage, hoping that you wouldn't wake up one morning and decide you'd made a mistake. Even now . . . I don't know why you married me, Tara."

His words were a plea, and as she gazed at him, Tara saw the wary look she had come to dread, an expression of half-angry vulnerability in his remarkable eyes. A sudden rush of almost painful love and tenderness swept over her, and she knew she would do anything—anything in her power—to wipe away that look on his face. She just couldn't bear to see exposed the chinks in her proud Devlin's armor. It was enough to know they were there.

Taking another giant step away from that frightened, defiant child who had ruled her emotions for so long, Tara said very quietly, "I love you, Devlin. I always have."

"You . . ." He seemed stunned, incapable of taking it in, his silvery eyes filling with a sudden glowing light that lit up all the remaining dark spots in Tara's heart.

She went to stand before him, no longer afraid, dimly aware that an aching wound inside her had finally healed. She was whole at last, the confession of her love binding woman and child together. She had never felt so alive. He could hurt her badly, she knew, send her scurrying back into the dark well she had only just climbed out of. But for this moment she didn't care. She was a woman, taking the same risk women down through the ages had always taken by loving a man, by placing her heart in his hands and her dreams at his feet.

"Tara, honey . . ." Suddenly, she was in his arms, being held as though he would never let her go, as if he would fight demons from hell to keep her. "I love you, sweetheart!" Rough hands turned her face up, stormy eyes glowed down at her just before his lips touched hers with an almost desperate need.

Tara met the kiss fiercely, glorying in her freedom, eager to show him how much she loved and needed him. Her arms slipped around his lean waist, her body molding itself to his hard, demanding length. Like a spark to dry kindling, she took fire in his arms.

Devlin drew away at last, but only far enough to rest his forehead against hers. "Good lord, you're combustible," he muttered hoarsely, half groaning and half laughing.

"You're not exactly a bucket of water yourself," she returned breathlessly.

He laughed unsteadily, molten fire still raging deep in his eyes. "You and I have a few things to discuss, Mrs. Bradley," he told her with mock sternness, "and I think we'd better talk now. I have a feeling we'll find better things to do with our time in the next few days."

"Days?" She widened her eyes innocently.

"Weeks. Years!" Laughing, he swept her up in his arms and carried her over to a chair, sitting down with her in his lap. In the gentle glow from a nearby lamp he smiled tenderly down at her. "Why didn't you tell me?" he asked softly.

"Tell *you?*" She traced a loving finger along his jaw. "I didn't even tell myself, at first. And then when I realized—"

"When?" he interrupted, catching her wandering fingers and carrying them briefly to his lips.

Tara smiled a little sheepishly. "It was . . . in Las Vegas, the day you came back from New York."

"That long ago?" His eyes flashed with a fleeting anger. "Damn it, why didn't you tell me sooner?"

She leaned forward to kiss him quickly, taking peculiar satisfaction in the fact that he could still get angry at her. "I was afraid to. I thought I was fighting for my life."

Devlin frowned. "I knew you were fighting something," he murmured, almost to himself. "All along you were fighting. At first I thought it was me. But we were so good together, I couldn't understand that. Then I thought you were fighting for your independence. It only dawned on me slowly that there was more to it than that."

"Much more." She smiled a little sadly and then quietly told him all about her childhood and what her parents' relationship had done to her. She made herself completely vulnerable to him, as she'd never done before.

When her voice trailed away at last, Devlin cupped her cheek in one large warm hand. "It was tragic that your parents had a bad marriage, and even more tragic that you had to suffer through it with them. And then to be shunted from one foster home to another . . ." He shook his head. "No wonder you were scared, afraid to trust."

Tara sighed softly. "I didn't understand myself. And I didn't know how you felt, which made everything worse."

"I'm surprised you didn't guess how I felt." He grimaced. "Everyone else did."

"I thought it was just an act! And you set me up so nicely with that fake engagement."

"There was no fake engagement."

"Would you repeat that?"

Devlin wound one of her bright curls around his finger and stared at it as though fascinated. "No fake engagement," he murmured almost absently. "It was completely real. Once I got my ring on your finger, I had every intention of keeping it there." His eyes slid sideways, filled with laughter and a hint of pleading. "I'm afraid you've been the victim of a plot, my love."

Tara's mouth fell open. "You mean—all along?"

"All along. I made up my mind to marry you, long before you collapsed."

Thinking back to all the fights and arguments they had had, she protested, "But you were always so angry at me. I thought it was hurt pride—because I'd refused to marry you."

"I know what you thought," Devlin told her dryly. "It was obvious from the first. But I've got news for you, love. A man doesn't seek out a woman for three years, *knowing* he's going to get a verbal slap in the face, just because she hurt his pride once upon a time."

Tara stared at him. "But what made you so determined then? Was it because I collapsed?"

"In a way." Devlin smiled. "After three years of fighting, I was afraid I just didn't have what it took to break through your barriers. But then, while you were sleeping so deeply in the hospital, you became very restless if I left the room. You'd cry out as if you were having nightmares. I was the only one who could quiet you. I knew then that I *had* broken through that wall. Something inside you needed me, trusted me."

"I can't believe you've loved me for so long," she whispered.

"Longer than you know. All along, in fact."

"You mean—?"

"I mean all along." He smiled crookedly. "I fell in love with you more than three and a half years ago. The night we met."

Astonished, Tara murmured, "I never guessed."

"It was a premiere party like any other," Devlin said quietly. "The same people, the same empty talk. I was bored stiff." His smile turned rueful. "And then lightning struck. Like a scene from a bad movie, the crowd parted and there you stood . . . a goddess."

Tara was half flattered, half amused. "You didn't think that!"

"I promise you I did." He grinned. "The most insane thoughts went through my mind. Helen of Troy. Diana. Lorelei. Venus. You were standing perfectly still, wearing a black gown, and you were different from every other woman in the room." His voice changed, deepened. "You looked so calm, so completely indifferent to the noise and the glamour and the famous actor who was talking to you. Like a statue carved from my dreams, so still and beautiful. Only the fire was missing."

Tara listened, half hypnotized by the quiet intensity of his voice, her heart thumping against her ribs.

"My view of you was blocked for a few seconds, and I was angry with all those faceless people for coming between us. And then I saw you again. The actor had said something to make you angry, and all of a sudden the fire was there. Your eyes were glittering, shooting sparks. Your face came to life. You turned on that actor with a sweet smile and maybe half a dozen words."

Tara's eyes widened as she recalled the moment. The actor had been talking for nearly an hour, name-dropping and using unsubtle lines older than he was. Tara had finally gotten fed up. Though she didn't remember her exact words, she had the distinct impression that her language had been less than ladylike.

Devlin was smiling. "I don't know what you said to him, but I've never seen a man deflate so quickly! Even with most of my attention on you, I saw him just melt away with an unnerved expression on his face. That's when I knew," he finished simply.

Feeling a bit unnerved herself, Tara managed a slight smile. "I'm surprised you didn't melt away like the actor," she murmured. "My temper—"

Devlin placed a gentle finger across her lips. "Your temper doesn't frighten me, honey," he said softly. "It never has. If anything, it delights me. It breathes fire into you, makes you real. As soon as I saw that, I was hooked."

Tara was suddenly, overwhelmingly aware that she must have hurt Devlin very badly by violently rejecting his first proposal. Holding his hand tightly, she said painfully, "And when you proposed . . . oh, darling, I'm so sorry! What you must have felt!"

Devlin smiled, his wry expression not quite hiding the pain in his eyes. "It wasn't . . . pleasant," he confessed quietly. "I was too angry to feel much of anything else for a while. Then I went out and got drunk—and stayed drunk for three days. I spent a lot of time staring at that damned ring and wondering what had gone wrong. And the hell of it was that I knew you wanted me."

He ran a gentle finger down her slightly flushed cheek. "That was something you could never hide from me," he murmured. "And in a lot of ways it was the worst part. I wanted more than just a lovely, passionate body in my bed. I wanted you—all of you—and it was hell, knowing that I could have your body but not your heart or your mind."

Devlin sighed. "I wrote that song about a month later. I thought it would help to get you out of my system . . . but it didn't. Nothing helped, really. I told myself to forget you, and that resolution lasted until I saw you again at some party. After that I found myself scheming like a besotted fool to be with you whenever I could. In a twisted sort of way, fighting with you was almost like making love to you."

"I wish I'd known," she whispered.

"I'm glad you didn't know," he told her ruefully. "That was the only thing that kept me sane—the fact that you didn't know how I felt about you. Sometimes we'd be arguing, and the sheer necessity of telling you how I felt would almost choke me."

Tara threw her arms around his neck and buried her face against his throat. "I've been such a fool," she said shakily. "Such a blind, stupid fool!"

He laughed unsteadily, his arms holding her tightly. "No, not a fool. Just confused and frightened. If I'd known that, it would have made things a lot easier. As it was, I just had to play it by ear. I got my ring on your finger and used every trick I could think of to make you aware of me, to make you need me."

Troubled, she murmured, "That night at Jim's apartment—you were so angry at me."

Devlin kissed her forehead gently. "Because you'd given me such a simple explanation of why we'd broken up. I couldn't believe you could have rejected me only because you thought I'd interfered

in your career. I was angry . . . and hurt. And bitter,
I suppose."

Tara lifted her head to stare at him gravely. "I
thought I'd made you hate me after that."

"You could never do that. By the next morning
I'd realized there had to be more to it than that.
And I knew I had my work cut out for me. So
I changed my attitude completely, determined to
keep you off guard and off balance. I thought if I
could just get you to the altar, we'd work all the
bugs out later."

Tara smiled at the phrase. "Were you hoping that
the Bradley 'luck' would help too?"

Devlin lifted her hand and gazed at the glittering
diamond beside the plain gold wedding band. "Jim
said he'd told you the story," he murmured. "I've
been wondering why you haven't asked me why I
was marrying you."

"I've asked you several times why you were so
determined to marry me," she said indignantly,
"why you were so convinced that we belonged
together. You always dodged my questions."

He grinned. "You didn't ask about the ring,
though. Didn't you wonder why I'd take a chance
and give that ring to a woman for any reason other
than love?"

Tara sighed. "The thought did cross my mind.
But your sneaky tricks worked so often that I was
usually too off balance to think clearly about anything. *Would* you have given the ring to a woman
you didn't love?" she asked curiously.

"No. But not because of the legend connected
with that ring." Devlin smiled crookedly. "I've never intended to marry for any reason except love.

And I never felt any desire to marry at all—until I met you."

She smiled at him, and then the smile died away. "You were so awful to me after that first night."

"Well, what did you expect?" He grimaced wryly. "We had just spent the night together—an experience, I might add, that I considered to be something dreams were made of—and you told me you'd made a mistake and didn't intend to repeat it! Was I supposed to cheerfully accept that and pretend not to be both hurt and angry?"

She touched his cheek in silent apology and felt her senses flare when he turned to kiss the soft inner flesh of her wrist. Trying to think clearly, she murmured, "You changed so quickly when I came out to the training ring that day. Why?"

"You didn't want to fight with me."

Tara looked blank. "And that meant . . . ?"

He chuckled. "Honey, when you refuse to fight with me, I *know* I'm getting somewhere!"

She stared at him. "Oh. So you decided the time was right for your bribe."

"Exactly. I knew you wouldn't be influenced by material things, but I hoped you'd eventually realize that a man doesn't present his woman with her dream house unless he cares very deeply."

"His woman?" Her voice was innocent.

"Of course." Devlin's eyes sparkled, "Since that very first night, we've belonged to each other."

"I'm glad you made that mutual. I'd hate to think I was just a possession."

Devlin surrounded her face with his large hands. "You are," he said very quietly, "my mind, my heart, and my soul. You're everything I ever wanted in a woman, everything I ever needed. With you beside me I feel . . . better than I am. I want nothing more than to spend the rest of my life with you."

Tara swallowed hard, her eyes filling with tears. "I love you, Devlin," she whispered.

He bent forward to kiss her tenderly. "I love you too, sweetheart," he murmured. "More than I'll ever be able to tell you."

"You're doing just fine," she said, hiccupping and laughing at the same time.

Devlin sat back, his hands sliding down to cup her throat warmly. "There's something I think I'd better confess," he murmured ruefully.

"What? More sneaky tricks?" she teased.

"No. At least, since it hasn't happened, it can't be called a trick." He sighed, then said baldly, "I hoped you'd get pregnant."

Tara's eyes widened, and she started to laugh in spite of herself. "You were going to trap me!"

Devlin smiled sheepishly. "Well, I wasn't counting on it, but I was hoping. I knew damn well you didn't want anything to interfere with your career, but—"

"My career," she murmured, interrupting him. "I've been meaning to talk to you about that. I'm committed to do *Celebration!* but after that . . . well, I'm not too old to change careers."

"What would you rather do?" he asked in an unsteady voice.

"Be with you," she said softly. "Every minute of every day and night. I want to raise children and horses. I want to go to sleep in your arms and wake up in your arms."

His throat moved in an almost convulsive swallow. "Are you sure, honey? I don't want you to regret anything," he said huskily.

"Very sure. By the way, are we going to sit down here talking all night? I thought we had better things to do with our time."

Devlin rose immediately to his feet with heart-stopping ease, still holding her in his arms. "I thought you'd never ask," he told her, striding toward the stairs.

Tara had thought there could be no surprises in their lovemaking, that it couldn't get better. But that night she discovered how wrong she could be—how wonderfully wrong.

Even if Devlin had mentioned no word of love, Tara would still have felt the love in him that night. For the first time they did not hold back or try to hide their feelings. Murmuring words of love and pleasure, they lost themselves in a world of magic.

As Devlin's lips moved hungrily toward the hardened tip of one breast, Tara wondered dizzily if she'd ever get used to this pleasure. And then his mouth captured her nipple, and she forgot everything but the spiraling tension inside of her. She returned his caresses eagerly, her fingers searching out all the secret places of pleasure. His husky groan spurred her on, and she continued her exploration, desperate to know every inch of his strong body, frantic to imprint the uncompromisingly male form in her mind and heart for all time. Like the wildcat he'd once humorously compared her to, she became a primitive creature in his arms.

For a while Devlin encouraged her fierce attempts to dominate their passionate struggle in the ages-old confrontation between man and woman. Switching roles with the ease of a man comfortable with and certain of his own masculinity, he allowed her the role of master, rolling over on his back and leaving himself vulnerable to her.

Dimly aware that she could control their love-making only because he allowed her to, Tara concentrated a certain power of her own into taking his breath away. She rained kisses on his face and neck, her hands moving teasingly over the hair-roughened chest, the flat stomach, and beyond. Exulting in his hoarse groans, she nibbled passionately on his ears and sank her teeth gently into the tanned flesh of his shoulders.

Their eyes clashed as she lifted her head, and Tara saw the molten flame in his gaze, telling her of limits reached and games done. He pulled her completely down on him, his hands guiding her body to fit his own, claiming her with gentle insistence and driving need. He controlled their heated movements with powerful ease, tension building between them until they reached the trembling peak together in a moment like the slow shattering of glass. And then the room became quiet and still.

Devlin's eyes searched Tara's intently as he pulled her down into the crook of his arm. Reading the question there, she smiled contentedly and snuggled up to him. She'd been a little worried herself that the nervous child inside of her might have surfaced again in the aftermath of their lovemaking, but that hadn't happened. Apparently woman and child were really one now. Tara had never felt so happy.

Falling asleep in his arms, she woke abruptly, late the next morning, sitting bolt upright in bed, her eyes snapping open. Her dreams flooded into her mind, and automatically she gazed down at Devlin's sleeping figure, stirring restlessly now that the warmth of her body had left his side.

She turned her gaze back to the sunlit room and frowned as a faint wave of nausea passed quickly. Her eyes widened suddenly as certain symptoms of the last few weeks began to add up. She held up one hand and carefully counted on her fingers, then stared across the room, a silly grin on her face.

Well, for goodness' sake! A grown woman, and she hadn't even realized what had happened!

Half turning, she stared down at Devlin's sleeping face, allowing herself a few moments just to look at him. Then, very deliberately, she picked up her pillow and hit him with it—not very hard, but it certainly woke him up. Before he could open his eyes, Tara mustered all her acting talents and produced a very creditable frown. "I've been wanting to hit you for years," she announced, glaring into his puzzled expression, "and I've finally thought of a good reason to!"

Pushing the pillow away, Devlin raised himself on one elbow and stared at her. "What *are* you talking about, witch?" he demanded, smothering a yawn with one hand.

"You and your plots." She sniffed disdainfully.

He fell back on his pillow with a faint groan and closed his eyes. "My dear wife," he murmured, "I have had an exhausting night and was short on

sleep to start with." He peered at her out of one
eye. "I have to admit, though, that the sight of your
delightfully bared assets is doing wonderful things
to my energy level."

Tara glanced down to discover that the blankets
had fallen to her waist. Frowning at him, she pulled
them hastily back up. "Stop changing the subject!"
she told him severely.

He opened the other eye. "The only subject I have
on my mind right now is you. Your punishment
for hitting me with that pillow is going to be very
involved and will probably cost me the rest of my
strength. Come here, you thorn in my flesh."

Tara evaded his seeking arms, keeping a death
grip on the blankets. "No. I want to talk to you, and
it isn't going to do you a bit of good to try to distract
me." When he tugged at the blankets playfully, she
tried to scoot away from him. "I mean it! You're not
going to—*Devlin!*"

"I'm not going to what?" he asked with interest.

Flat on her back, Tara stared up at him. "That's
not fair. You're bigger than I am!" she complained.

Devlin loomed over her, grinning cheerfully and
neatly disposing of the blankets. "Something I
intend to take shameless advantage of, darling,"
he told her softly, his fingers threading through
her red curls. "I am an opportunist, after all."

"You certainly are," she managed breathlessly,
trying to ignore the lips moving slowly down her
throat. "Oh, lord—if this is the way you plan to end
all our arguments, I'm licked before I start!"

He lifted his head, his silvery eyes grown dark
and stormy. "Were we having an argument?" he
murmured. "I can't seem to remember."

"I think we were going to," she replied weakly, and then muttered, "Oh, hell . . ." and pulled his mouth back down to hers.

The sun had climbed higher in the sky when Tara finally stirred again. Her husband's arms drew her even closer, and she smiled faintly. "You always get what you want, don't you, Devlin Bradley?" she asked in a wry tone.

"Always," he agreed complacently. "Some things just take longer, that's all. But I'm a patient man."

"Shameless. You are absolutely shameless." She rolled over, resting her chin on the hands folded atop his chest. "Between your plotting and the infamous Bradley luck, you had things pretty well sewn up, didn't you?"

He ran a gentle finger down her nose. "You gave me a few uncertain moments," he said dryly. "I was determined to win, though."

"Well, I hope you knew what you wanted," she told him calmly, "because you got it all."

Devlin stared at her. "I get the feeling," he commented, "that you're leading up to something."

"I always knew you were smart."

He reached down to swat her lightly. "Stop being sassy and tell me the reason for that very unnerving gleam in your eyes!"

Tara laughed delightedly. "Is it unnerving? Wonderful! I'd hate to think you were utterly sure of yourself."

"Tara, my love," he said carefully, "if you don't tell me what's on that maddening mind—" He broke off abruptly and frowned. "Why did you hit me with that pillow, anyway?"

She gave him a serene smile. "Because it suddenly occurred to me that all your plotting and scheming couldn't have worked out better—for you—if the whole thing had been a chess game with me as the pawn." Tracing a finger over his chin, she went on conversationally, "You remember that scene in *Celebration!* where Maggie sings your song?"

He nodded. "I remember."

Tara's smile widened. "Well, if you'll remember, Maggie is pregnant in that scene. We'll have to film that scene first . . . and I won't need a pillow."

Devlin went very still, his darkened eyes searching her face. "Tara?" he breathed questioningly.

No longer able to contain the happiness bubbling up inside her, she pulled herself forward to kiss him. "I think you said you wanted a girl," she murmured huskily. "And wanted to name her something Irish."

"Something Irish," he repeated, dazed. "Tara, honey, are you sure? And—you don't regret its happening so soon?"

"As sure as I can be without going to a doctor. And I'm not the least bit sorry. Are you?"

"My God, don't even ask!" he rasped huskily, drawing her even closer. "It's what I've wanted all along—you and our children. I love you, sweetheart . . ."

"My darling Devlin . . ."

Quite a while later Tara finally roused herself enough to murmur, "Um . . . there's something I'd better tell you. I don't have any living relations, but, well . . . both my parents were twins. And you know what they say about twins skipping a generation."

"You mean—?"

"I mean it's something to think about." She cuddled closer to him. "With the Bradley luck sitting in your corner . . . and you said you wanted at least four kids . . . don't you think we'd better consider enlarging the nursery, just in case?"

14 ALL NEW TALES OF DEATH AND DESIRE
FROM TODAY'S TOP MYSTERY WRITERS

CRIMES

OF THE

HEART

Lia Matera	edited by	Joan Hess
Nancy Pickard	Carolyn	Margaret Maron
P.M. Carlson	G. Hart	Dorothy Cannell
Susan Dunlap		Carolyn G. Hart
D.R. Meredith		Sharyn McCrumb
Audrey Peterson		Jeffery Wilds Deaver
Marilyn Wallace		Barbara D'Amato

___ 0-425-14582-4/$9.00